THE OTHER WATCH

By

Henry S. Whittier

TO: Don

Henry S. Whittier

Published 2000 by
Medicine Label Press
Rural Route # 2
West Bay, Nova Scotia
B0E 3K0

Whittier, Henry S. (Henry Sayward), 1924-
    The other watch

ISBN 0-9693058-5-0

    1. Saladin (Ship)–Fiction. 2. Mutiny–Nova Scotia–
Fiction. 3. Trials (Piracy)–Nova Scotia–Halifax–Fiction.
I. Title.

PS8595.H4983O84 2000   C813'.6   C00-900785-7
PR9199.3.W4586Ot 2000

Front cover: design and drawing by Andru Lordly
Back cover: photo by Bob Martin

Printed and bound in Canada
City Printers Limited, Sydney, Nova Scotia

DEDICATION

To the reader: "The gift of reading–as I have called it, is not very common, nor very generally understood. It consists, first of all, in a vast intellectual endowment–a free grace, I find I must call it–by which a man rises to understand that he is not punctually right, nor those from whom he differs, absolutely wrong. He may hold dogmas; he may hold them passionately; and he may know that others hold them but coldly, or hold them differently, or hold them not at all. Well, if he has the gift of reading, there are others that will be full of meat for him."

R.L. S.

ACKNOWLEDGMENTS

I wish to thank Kai Lehrke, my friend and computer guru, who guided me through the jungle of book preparation with patience and intrepidity. I also wish to thank my editor and publisher, Wilf Cude, whose patience and skilled reading led to encouragement and the eventual publication of this work. And thanks are also due to my wife, Pearl, for her loving editorial work throughout.

EPIGRAPH

Nel mezzo del cammin di nostra vita
mi ritrovai per una selva oscura,
che la diritta via era smarrita.

Ahi quanto a dir qual era e cosa dura
questa selva selvaggia ed aspera e forte,
che nel persier rinnova la paura!

Inferno I, 1-6

PREAMBLE

A Find

This tale, event, experience–name it as you like–was told in the forties of the last century by a man who, by his own confession, was thirty years old at the time. Thirty is not a bad age–unless seen in perspective, when no doubt it is contemplated (by the majority of us at a more advanced age) with mixed feelings. It is a trying age; standing aside, we older ones begin to remember what fine men we used to be. Most people at thirty have begun to take a somewhat distorted view of themselves. Even their failures exhale a peculiar charm. The hopes of the future are fine company to live with, exquisite forms, idealistic if you like.

I suppose it was the idealism of increasing age which set our man to relate his experience for his own satisfaction; it could not have been for his glory, because the experience was one of profound doubt; terrifying ambiguity, he calls it. Perhaps it would not be difficult for a reader to guess that the relation between experience and satisfaction alluded to in the very first lines of his notes would be found in his text.

This writing constitutes the "Find," stated as a possible sub-title. The title itself is my own contrivance (I call it invention) and has the merit of veracity.

The "Find" was made in a box of books bought in Halifax from a second-hand bookseller in the last state of decay. As the books themselves, on inspection, turned out to be not worth the small amount of cash I spent, it must have been some premonition of that fact which made me say, "But I must have the box too."

A litter of loose pages at the bottom of the box excited my curiosity. The close, neat handwriting was not attractive at first sight. But in one place the statement that in 1844 the writer WAS thirty years of age caught my eye; that, and in addition, his assertion that he was a teacher of literature and philosophy.

Thirty years old is an interesting age in which one is easily reckless and a willing exponent of an ideal of justice, in spite of the fates which are well known to teachers, such as Socrates and Sir Thomas More; the growing faculty of reflection and the power of imagination are yet strong. Some snatches of sea-going phrases and references to mutiny further excited my interest: how might teaching and seafaring be reconciled in one man's adventures? Curiosity led me on to put in order the papers I had found.

Oh, but it was a dull-faced MS, each line resembling every other in close-set, regular order. It was like the drone of a monotonous voice. A treatise on the meaning of justice (the dreariest subject I can think of) could have given a livelier appearance. "Some accounting is necessary. I must begin this and finish it," and so the author begins earnestly from the Golden Inn in Lunenburg in 1844. While I enjoyed the thorny sort of datedness of the language, don't imagine there is anything archaic in my find. Ingenuity in invention, though as old as the world, is by no means a lost art. Look at the telephones for shattering the little peace of mind given us in this world or at automatic rifles or ICBMs for letting life out of our bodies. Now-a-days any blear-eyed serial killer strong enough to pull a trigger or push a button could lay low any number of us in the blink of an eye.

If this isn't progress!...why, it's absolutely terrific! We have moved on, and so you must expect to meet here a certain naivete of contrivance and simplicity of aim arising from a remote time. And of course no tourist, prisoner of a Winnebago, can hope to find a public hanging of mutineers now. This one was situated in Halifax. The writer seems to have entered into most elaborate detail of the why and wherefore of his presence at that trial and execution. I found that his experience has nothing to do with the sea, though the sea has its place in his adventure, being a part of his envisioned account of what led to the denouement, that is, the last public hanging in Halifax. A careful explanation of all the circumstances was to be expected from our man, only, I gather, some of his pages may very well be missing: gone in covers for jam-pots or stuffing for boxes packed for shipping. Thus some of the details can only be inferred from the preserved scraps of his conscientious writing and thinking as he reconstructs for his listener (readers) the events leading up to the execution, events which he, apparently, gleaned from newspaper accounts of the trial including the confessions of the various mutineers.

Finally, I found my interest most fully nourished in our man's wrestling with (if not ever pinning his understanding of) the workings of authority as exercised and sometimes even found in law and the law's workings toward what is sometimes called justice. Perhaps Soloman Scharf's ideal was to ask the question of himself: "what is law?"–and perhaps to give himself by his MS (and us in a careful reading of it) an answer?

CHAPTER ONE

The Execution

I make the above declaration because I fear to die without disclosing the truth; no man knows how soon he may die. **A steward's confession.**

The Golden Inn, Lunenburg, 6 August, 1844: Some accounting is necessary. I must begin this again and finish it, and I will by the only means left to me–a journal, a man's final access to what he feels to be the truth. I am a patient listener and a penetrating questioner, undergoing the trials of a long voyage with a fortitude that Abraham Cunningham himself might admire. It will soon end, if end it will–and mine is the voice one may hear crying in the wilderness, perhaps of my own making. And it is a voice driven onward, all the same, by wind and sea to that harbouring rock on which l run aground called security, a name that is not without irony for me. My arrival here and the voyage I record are not without parallel. A man whose personal concerns seek certainty, as well as the teacher who only asks that the man pause long enough in his search to see himself searching and seeking in this present accounting as valuable a treasure as the knowledge he seeks and to grasp as well the authority such a desire for possession holds over the would-be grasper. Yes, a teacher and food and ale in the man–the possessed and the possessor, or, at least, so it seems–the opposite may sometimes be the case, and, once again, the dilemma, the trial is mine. A taste of the public room of a hostelry in this my native town before sitting down in the rented room to write makes an appropriate refuge from what I see as the desert preceding it, perhaps, but the form and the arrangement the public room took calls to mind other rooms and other voices. I looked toward the back of the room to the bar; behind it a serving table and panelled door gave a narrow glimpse into the kitchen; on my left, the round tables stood where food and drink are arraigned, tried and judged by a hungry jury of guests. On my right, across the room, the table on which the accused was waiting, steaming silently, to be served sentence. And behind the bar the barman dispensed liquors that enhance the appetite and befog the judgment, leaving not a few jurymen all at sea. But the chief justice was unseen, hidden yet presiding, and all here–master, guest and servant–were his shadows whose lives depended on our willing recognition of his Law and his sentence. We heard it in the kitchen in the sounds of cleaver and ladle, plate and bowl and glass, fork and knife; we heard it in the scraping chair, the rattling knife on the table or plate, muttering voices and muffled belch, even in the knock of a glass set down. Yes, a busy and prosperous inn speaks aloud to the ear that hears, and the voice is the voice of judgment. I hear it still, I confess, sitting here alone in my room, a self-appointed counsel for the defense, brief completed, waiting to begin his summation, listening to the voice of judgment which sounds in my ears, my defensive argument perhaps somewhat unusual.

The defense is the confession I write here, a confession that seems well-nigh suicidal, perhaps, acknowledging as it seems the predominance of our animal nature. This is a judicial decree if there ever was one, based upon a voluntary confession as circumspect as has ever been made. And not entirely unrelated in its way to the confessions of the six survivors of the *Saladin* with whom I share my fate. The formal statements of confession first came to my knowledge in *The Morning Post*. They had, at first, persisted in their original story told to Cunningham on the *Saladin's* decks. But on the 8th of June the Attorney-General, the Honourable James William Johnston, received a message from Carr–the *Saladin's* cook–and Galloway, his steward, requesting the Attorney-General to come to the jail at 9 p.m. that evening, a Saturday. It seemed they wished to confess. What subsequently occurred could have taken the following form, so it seems to me.

At Johnston's request, J.J.Sawyer, the High Sheriff, with Michael Tobe (the Lloyd's agent who sailed to Drumhead on the *Fair Rosamund* with Abraham Cunningham) to act as witness, went to the jail to hear the expected confessions. Johnston told the Sheriff he would join them later. The two met; it was cloudy and dark, the wind rising as they proceeded to the jail located in Halifax contiguous to the Poor House Burying Grounds off Albermarle Street near Grafton. A repeated knock at the outer door brought the jailer on duty to admit them, first to the narrow entrance hall and then through an iron grating serving as a door into a whitewashed central space. A polished oaken table was placed in the centre of this area. Four iron cell doors, a small sliding panel in each allowing the jailer to see into the cell, appeared to the left and right. A door in the wall opposite the entrance gave access to the jailer's quarters. It was closed. Sawyer and Tobe sat down at the table; the Law and Assurance awaited the prisoner's tale. The jailer, after peering through the access panel, unlocked the first cell door on the left. Carr emerged; he looked like one suffering from sleeplessness and fear, one that sought relief in any way he could from his present state. He sat down opposite Sawyer and handed a written confession to him. The jailer stood behind him, the ring holding his keys hanging from his belt, as the High Sheriff glanced through the document in his hand, nodding silently, and returned it to the prisoner. "Read it," he said.

Carr began to read in a voice I seem to hear still, a voice resonant and forceful, but marked by unctuous piety. "It is by the blessing of God that I am come here. I have told some lies in order to conceal the things which have occurred, but I now wish to tell the truth in order to relieve my mind." Relieve his mind! This is the man who couldn't rest until Captain Fielding was overboard, Carr's captain, whom he voluntarily agreed to serve in his pious recognition of Fielding's and Carr's God: security in the guise of command. Carr had seen salvation in following this captain's command; but as his voice droned on, the confession rested on the cook's innocent fear for his life. It was once again the morning after a night of carnage; Carr had seen Moffat's blood on the deck and on the galley door. While it is true that he might well fear for his life, it is also true that he embraced the incarnation of death as a protection, a source of security! Innocent as he was, but hardly in the sense he attempted to establish. He was ordered, nay, coerced into following Fielding; his commander was the fear of death, the twin brother of the desire to survive, heavenly twins like *Apollo* and *Artemis*, but pagans still. The other watch, the other authority– what of that? What of the voice which, ironically echoing Fielding's life-long motto, spoke, or might have spoken to Carr as he faced Fielding that Sunday morning on the quarterdeck above him–*non serviam*–the authentic voice of Carr himself as a man loving his life and therefore all life? He silenced the voice by serving the new captain he had chosen–and silencing that living voice was his death, I swear it. He looked into the eyes of death and gave his service, soul and body, to it. But it was this same death-defying cook who, eighteen hours later, learned of the hidden twin threat, two horse-pistols concealed by his chosen captain. And so, once again, and for the first time, he acted on Fielding's *non serviam:* he and the wooden-legged man Jones threw Fielding overboard. Carr's authentic voice spoke in this deed, but it was once again heard and seen as fear, fear for his life. He is, it seems, forced to eat his own cooking.

And now his voice was bringing confession to the ears of the High Sheriff and the Lloyd's agent–in order to relieve his mind, for God's sake! This confession, this tale, to my mind, is Carr's final deed which sums up all the rest. By confessing, he tacitly gave himself and his life to the authority outside himself. The Carr that died in the oath he gave to serve Fielding only lived again by the murder of his chosen captain–this was his harbour island refuge, although he may not have known it at the Line. The death and life of William Carr became, through confession, his source of life in a Halifax jail. His word, like the axes wielded by some of his well-fed shipmates, cut him off from the dying self who joined Fielding and that other living self who cut the captain off. His word was his deed–and so he lived in his confession as he lived his life, as we all spend our lives in pious worship of security and obedience to its Law; my journal is no exception. The confession, as I see it, recreates the crime and sets the creator inside it and outside it, at the same time. What authority could or would find a cook the likes of Carr guilty? And of what crime? Murder? Yes, but the murder of rational analysis, of reason itself and the man who lives by its dictates, regarding reason alone as his Creator whose light reveals reason to be only a shadow of His life-giving act. This light and this shadow, life and reason, reveals itself in the cook's tale–my tale. Yes, Carr had once again given his life into the hands of what he saw as security embodied in the persons of Sawyer and Tobe seated in the jail listening to the cook's voice. It yet remains to see what the authority of the Supreme Court, the seat of reason, would perform, would articulate, in the case of this cook. His final words, perhaps, image forth most clearly what seems my final word in his case: "The watch given up by me was the property of Captain MacKenzie; I have another which belonged to George Moffat. I make this disclosure because I cannot die with such a burthen on my mind, and I am perfectly ready to abide by the laws of my country." And then he signed his name below which the Sheriff and Tobe signed theirs. The watches of MacKenzie and Moffat–those members, captain and ordinary seaman, of the other watch left their watches to a mutinous cook who now became the time-server he had shown himself to be before–he was, indeed, abiding by the laws of his country!

The jailer returned the cook to his cell, a redundant act, it seems. The lock's heavy click followed the door's heavy clang, and the jailer looked through the panel into the dark cell beside the cook's, opened the door, and John Galloway emerges. The young Irishman blinked in the dim light as he was guided to the seat Carr had vacated. As Carr had, he carried a written confession that he handed to Sawyer. His experiences seemed to have left no visible mark upon him; even a slight sign of amusement flickered in the steward's gray eyes as they watched Sawyer's face while the Sheriff glanced over the confession in his hand. It was returned to him with the words, "Read it!"

The steward's voice, like the cook's, was strong and determined. He, too, it seems, saw himself as having been coerced into mutiny. The steward who had become navigator under Johnston's command followed Carr's star to a harbour island to which the Law of survival directed him in spite of his inept calculations. His tale varied from the cook's only in his claims to innocence; when ordered to help throw Fielding overboard, he had refused. When his life was threatened because of the refusal, he had laid his hands on Fielding while the cook and Jones had done their duty. That laying on of hands endowed the captain the steward had sworn to serve with a spiritual office. To the authority to whom he had served food as a steward he now gave a holy office. His hand, his touch, had made the man he touched a god, and that god was the death that the steward had formerly given his allegiance to by his oath on the cook's *Bible*. The steward's innocence was not of the order his confession tried to affirm; his thought, like his navigation, was faulty. He had lost that innocence over the stern at the moment he decided, for fear of losing his life, to follow Fielding's authority–or had he lost it? He was deaf to the authentic voice, but the voice went on to be heard now as it was then in the jail. Perhaps his attempt to drown that voice is best seen in the steward's and cook's subsequent action: these two, purveyors of food and drink to the authority they served, threw their captain's son, Joseph Fielding, over the side. Before the boy disappeared, he tried to save himself by seizing the steward's shirt. It tore away in his hand and the boy went overboard. The steward gave his now-unforced hand to the cook in murdering the boy; thus he did everything in his power to destroy his innocence, only to reveal in the murder the innocence he sought to kill.

And now, echoing the cook, his confession acknowledged his crime, his action on the *Saladin* in performing which he judged and attempted to condemn himself to the death he swore to serve, and then acted on that oath. At first with his hand on the captain and then stripped of a part of his clothing, by the hand of the boy he killed. As he had then, he now sought security under the Law of survival by affirming his crime once again in the ears of the Law's agents–who would perhaps concede him his guilt when the *Saladin's* actions wouldn't. The Supreme Court might perform the rite and save his guilt and his innocence too. A sin in the cook's case, the authentic voice speaks through the steward's as well. His final words sound the note: "I make the above declaration because I fear to die without disclosing the truth; no man knows how soon he may die." And then he signed his name to the death-warrant that would give him his life; Tobe and Sawyer were adding their names to the document when a muffled metallic sound was heard from a cell behind the High Sheriff exactly opposite the steward's. At the same time, a heavy knocking sounded at the outside door, which the jailer chose to answer first. The Attorney-General, William Johnston, entered and took his seat at the head of the table, briefly excusing himself for being late. He had been detained at the dinner by James Uniacke, Lawrence Doyle and George Young, attorneys for the defense in the *Saladin* case. While he was speaking, the sound from the cell ceased as the jailer looked into it through the sliding panel. He listened to the prisoner's whispered request and complied by unlocking the cell door. Emerging from the darkness, William Johnston stepped boldly forward, confession in hand, and sat down facing his namesake, the Attorney-General, at the opposite end of the table.

Identical in name only, apparently, the red-haired ex-commander of the *Saladin* , blue-eyed, muscular and tanned, contrasted strongly with the dark-eyed, black-haired, ruddy-cheeked Attorney-General, whose broad shoulders and expansive belly spoke of his legal success. Present Law and past captain stared intensely at one another in unbroken silence. Before Johnston handed his confession roughly to the High Sheriff on his left, he spoke, explaining that he and three other prisoners had conferred together when they could, having to wait the opportunity given by their jailer's temporary absences, whispering from cell to cell. Johnston, Jones, Hazleton and Anderson had originally planned to hold to the story they told Captain Cunningham; Carr and Galloway agreed. But following an examination they had undergone that morning, during which they held to their original tale, the cook and steward, suffering from the so-called timidity they had shown before, swore they intended to confess all. The cook then prepared the message that, delivered, had brought Sawyer, Tobe and now Johnston to the jail. The four, coerced by yet another threat to their lives, could do nothing but follow the cook and steward, their one-time servants. Each of the four had prepared a written statement, therefore, but it was yet to be seen whether each would submit his confession. Johnston himself, partially overhearing the cook's and steward's voices as they read their statements, must have seen himself, suddenly, in a new light. Yes, he would confess and so make his as-yet secret deed an open actuality. One can readily see his similarity to the cook and steward in the sense of life he found in the desperate attempt to make his killing lack of respect for life a reality, his own life as well as others' lives which are indeed one. The authority to which he submitted, sitting before him, embodied and bearing his name, would be willing to accept his need, acquiescing in his tacit request as it had for cook and steward.

The *Saladin's* third commander began his judgment by passing the confession to the Attorney-General who glanced at it. He returned it saying, "Read it, Johnston, and remember, there is nothing either to be promised you or to threaten you with; what you say must be said only from a desire to speak the truth." Ominous word, when I recall what Johnston meant by the truth, or the desire to speak it. The two men image forth an alarming identity: one wielded an axe at the other's unsolicited request for it–if we agree to confess that authentic voice and event transpiring in the jail before our eyes. The prisoner's voice was hoarse and unnaturally loud: "William Johnston is the name I shipped by, but my right name is William Trevaskiss. I was born in London. The first commencement of the mutiny, as I call it, though it was more like murder than mutiny, our cook was sick, and I was taken for cook one day. While I was cook, I had this plot made up to me by George Jones. He told me what he and Captain Fielding had made up between them, and the best thing I could do was to go on their side for my own safety." So all the ingredients are once again heard in Johnston's opening words. He was of the cook's party without knowing it–a safety seeker who, like cook and steward in this at least, allowed *Artemis*, or desire for survival, to take his life, while *Apollo*, or the fear of death, stood by bow in hand. Johnston gave himself into death's hands in the name of salvation–a cook if there ever was one. But, I notice, Johnston is not his name! Hence, perhaps, he can only be seen as an acting cook, although he did fulfil that role on board the *Saladin*. The man was two men if in the name only; he who joined Fielding through fear was Johnston, while Trevaskiss, the other watch, was hidden but seeing–just as the cook's and steward's authentic voice was drowned when they exchanged life for safety. "I was forced then to side with them to save my own life," said the prisoner as his confession continued. Johnston, the alias, the shadow, the name saves that spectral life at the expense of Trevaskiss who, unseen, lives on, a victim of the axe of choice, an embodiment of what he lost through this self-sacrifice. The cook, it seems, was sick; Jones "made up the plot" to Johnston–but who was Jones, really, if not the voice in which Trevaskiss heard himself called Johnston? And he said he called it mutiny, though it was more like murder than mutiny! My God, how clearly men don't see! how revealing their blindness is sometimes!

The prisoner' voice read on; he seemed, by his own account, to be absent from the events he told Johnston, Sawyer and Tobe of–absent–in other words, not present. It is, is it not, an accurate delineation of Trevaskiss, perhaps? As cook and steward died in giving their allegiance to Fielding, or security, or death, so did Johnston, but with this difference–Trevaskiss was absent, apparently. But Johnston acted his part on the *Saladin* that night, absent or not. He decapitated the first mate with an axe, saw Hazleton and Anderson return from MacKenzie's cabin scared off by, of all things, a dog! And then, a detail that clearly stuck in the prisoner's mind, he heard, and still hears as he confessed, Captain MacKenzie's bell ringing three times–no one to answer–three times, a catholic signal common to us all. The call that makes food live, and shows us to be the cannibals into which we apparently make ourselves, not unlike the acting cook did when he fed on the headless mate to nourish his desire to live and, eventuof ally, to command. Perhaps unlike the cook and steward, this acting cook fed on the first mate, using the mate's substantial body to embody his, the acting cook's, dream of survival. A headless mate made him first into a first mate himself under Fielding, and, finally, with Fielding's apparent departure–for what else was it–the acting cook became the third captain of the *Saladin*! Trevaskiss alias Johnston alias Fielding alias MacKenzie–an unusual chain of command, isn't it? And their ship, the *Saladin*, ruled them all in the role of Security, their mutual Harbour Island in the country in which they all chose to harbour their lives. Johnston-Trevaskiss commanded the *Saladin* in a sense in which MacKenzie, Fielding, Johnston and Cunningham never could because he was two men, not one; and so, much like us, apparently he couldn't command at all–the Law and the voice that affirms itself in the very articulation of an apparently absolute denial. Johnston lived by killing and so killing became his life, his living; while Trevaskiss lived on, an accessory after the fact and our legal cooks might serve it up.

The prisoner's confessing voice still sounded in Johnston's ears, as it did in the others' as well. The absence he professed in his account of the events on the *Saladin* more and more strongly affirmed his presence, Trevaskiss's presence, in the jail at this communion table. The recognition of the Law, the authority whose representatives heard his works, established, as it had for the cook and steward before him, the actuality of his guilt and his complicity–and, therefore, the actuality of the Trevaskiss Johnston had made him. Living through killing, this death brought him to life–Trevaskiss's voice and the words that give it body also gave witness to his life, a creature of His Creator of whom he was the image–Captain Johnston. The words to be heard in the Supreme Court would nourish Trevaskiss and Captain Johnston slowly faded away to the shadow he was in reality.

The voice ceased, the hand signed "William Johnston"

at the end of his last chapter; the three signed below the prisoner's signature–W. Johnston, J. Sawyer and M. Tobe. The jailer returned his charge to the darkened cell, the iron door closed with a heavy clang and Trevaskiss was alone once again with Johnston, the stubborn member of the other watch. It was midnight and the three witnesses, spell-bound by what they had heard, sat silent for a long moment. "Well, that should simplify my task," said Johnston, "and give me the blessing of a short trial–the Attorney-General is the guardian of the living Law, and his task isn't always made easy by confession. In the hope that others will follow suit soon, I bid you good night." With this, Johnston stepped into the darkness, the iron door closing heavily behind him. Sawyer soon followed with Tobe, who had carefully picked up the confessions and placed them in his leather case for safe keeping. The jailer, alone now with his confessed and unconfessed prisoners, secures the outer doors before he extinguished the overhead light and withdrew into the darkness of his own cell. He was the steward of the legal kitchens awaiting the provender that would indeed provide a courtly feast if Johnston received the answer his hopes signified.

******

Sawyer and Tobe received a message from the jailer requesting them to appear at the jail at noon the day following the first night of confession. It seemed that Hazleton and Anderson were on deck, ready to die for the country in which they chose to live, ready, that is, to mutiny in the name of the Law. The High Sheriff and the Lloyd's agent gained admittance to the jail to see Hazleton already seated before them at the table at which they had dined the previous night. His written confession was in hand, and he began to read aloud in a voice lacking the determination I seem to have heard in the cook's and steward's, or the unnaturally loud and hoarse tones

the acting cook. Hazleton's voice showed unconcern, even indifference. Black eyes, hair and beard, and a swarthy complexion enhanced by his characteristic red kerchief and black open shirt, made him appear the piratical being he apparently was. Here was the first of the lesser lights among the prisoners; the three cooks had the twins of security, desire and fear, those two horse-pistols, to give them the means to achieve their choice. Hearing Hazleton's voice as he began, it became clear that his feeling was different from that of his predecessors. If they sought to possess a dream, namely security, he sought nothing but the money he might gain; he, like the gold, showed a marked propensity to seem as indifferent as only gold can be–Midas was, after all, only a pirate in king's clothing which failed to keep his secret. "I was in the galley when Jones proposed to me that our watch should take possession of the vessel for the sake of the money on board." He, unlike the three cooks, was, in a sense, apparently dead already. If this was indeed his case, his part in the killing would be difficult, for how on earth can one kill a ghost?

With this man it was not the case of drowning or silencing the authentic voice; he simply was stone deaf to it, deaf as the gold he coveted and lived for. "That night Captain Fielding came on deck and asked me, (I believe all–he asked me) if we were all ready–for that night it ought to be done." To this prisoner all were one with him, spectral beings under Fielding, the figure of the death which saves, the death which rewards, the non-being of security. Hazleton was indeed his captain's man. In the role of Johnston's first mate, Hazleton made a suitable second, appointed as he was by Fielding later, after their oath on the cook's *Bible*. The deaths of MacKenzie and Moffat were in part this man's acts; he committed the murders without compunction because to him those he slaughtered were, like him, already gone. You see, his part in Captain MacKenzie's death was like the steward's part in the murder of Fielding's son: the outward and visible sign of an inward and material damnation; being, the authentic voice seemingly silenced, was this pirate's love of money.

The prisoner's voice droned indifferently on. He told of his and Anderson's descent into MacKenzie's cabin to kill the man on their captain's orders. "We said yes. And there was a dog lying alongside the captain's berth; and we said when we came on deck we were afraid the dog might bite us." What did Hazleton, the indifferent seeker after gold, see in that brown dog? Wasn't it a living being of which he was afraid? What was it he feared? It was, it seems, the living reminder of Hazleton himself, recalling in appearing thus before the man's eyes his own life, transform it as he would into gold, alchemist as he was. And that dog guarded MacKenzie's life and, however briefly, saved it. The man feared the dog's bite– a sign of his animal sense of survival, not unlike the dog's that barred his act. Self-condemned as he was, once again I hear the authentic voice in this, faint though it may seem. If the three cooks prepared the food that their ghosts ate in confession, Hazleton's were the canine teeth that made the food swallowable. Through the dog we see the man. He went on to uncover a marked similarity to Johnston; he, like his next-to-last captain, was apparently absent, asserting his distance from the central incidents on the *Saladin* that night. Ironic that a man who tries to reduce his life to a dog's should seek exoneration from his crime by asserting his absence! He recalled his and Johnston's murder of Moffat beside the galley and said, "I was afraid that if I did not strike, Johnston would strike me." Murder, it seems, is its own defense; and the desire for survival is its reason, its justification–an interesting possibility, isn't it?

The early afternoon sun shone through a high western window in the confessional. The elongated shadows of the two men appeared on the table, meeting at a point just short of Hazleton's seated figure but shading the page from which he read. His eyes saw the two shadows made one in his

fession. He, too, sought desperately for safety in self-sacrifice, in his death seeking the gold of life, the perhaps unwilling but surely unconscious witness for the voice he could not hear. His closing words will bear this out: "We divided the money, and when the ship struck we put it all in a chest to land it more readily." First and last, the money, Hazleton's life. "When Captain Cunningham came on board we asked for a Consul or some person to take charge." The last captain of the *Saladin* was Cunningham, whom her crew hoped would save them and return what they had denied with word and axe. Sawyer and Tobe were suitable answers to such a plea.

Anderson materialized in Hazleton's place at the table, the latter having been returned to the inner darkness to count the gold he sought. The Swede's swarthy skin, fiery eyes and dark hair belied his nationality, those fair-haired Scandinavians. He was asked to read the confession. As he began in a cold, dry voice, his origins became clear–he spoke in a thick Swedish accent and while his English was good, his articulation made it difficult to catch. He was a foreigner, but not only in the common sense of that over-used word; he seemed an alien spirit, isolated and alone in a world, whether ship or cell, in which he does not belong. The fire in his eyes spoke his profound hatred of authority in any form as his confession revealed. "There were fourteen persons on board the *Saladin* when we left Valparaiso; six of them are here–eight of them are not here: they were killed." To Anderson, it seems, the tale was simple–just a matter of mathematics; fourteen minus eight leaves six! Two months of sailing, braving Cape Horn itself in the course of it, is apparently unworthy of notice in Anderson's eyes. He sailed from Valparaiso to the Line in mid-Atlantic, but that voyage, that time, doesn't exist for him. And what of the events on the *Saladin*? He recounted the distribution of axe and maul, hammer and adze, among Captain Fielding's crew. He saw Johnston kill the mate and told of accompanying Hazleton to MacKenzie's cabin to kill him but "we returned for fear of the dog." Hazleton feared getting bitten, but Anderson feared the dog–the Swede, it would seem, is Hazleton's shade. Hazleton loved money and feared the dog's teeth; Anderson wanted revenge: "By God, I'll take a knife and cut his throat. He shall no more strike me from the helm!" was his oath of allegiance to Fielding. Revenge and fury, the shadow arising from and following implicit and savage revenge on the authentic voice, or life itself, for its apparent failure to submit to possession, to the hands of the lover of money. Anderson was the ghost that in many ways sums up the one force all those would-be mutineers obeyed–the desire for security and the fear of death which they all acted upon–and Fielding, their shadowy commander, whose ascendency was maintained by the central threat. The other watch will kill if they did not kill first themselves. And of course, it did.

The Swede, like his avaricious counterpart, Hazleton, was deaf to the authentic voice, not because he attempted to drown or kill it, but simply because he was an apparently disembodied spirit without feeling or senses–the spectre of life that arose after the mutineers had exchanged life for safety. Ironically, the Swede was their safety as their chosen action had created it–he was the Law of security itself, walking among them, killing without apparent feeling Allen and Collins outright, and the Ship's Carpenter and MacKenzie with Hazleton and Jones and Fielding. It was the Swede, also, who exposed Fielding's plot to kill four of his sworn crew. This occurred at the time Johnston discovered the hidden horse-pistols. Together, their evidence condemned Fielding to death; he was executed by the cook and Jones, the sail-maker and acting steward. Anderson was an authentic killer like death itself. He lived to die, and death, for him, was the beginning of a life he seemed to seek in the midst of life itself. His confession is the shortest of all the six; his terrifying ability to distil the events on the *Saladin* and his part in them is the conmeasure of his coldness, the coldness that images forth the undying fiery heat of his desire for revenge. Once again I ask myself how the Law could condemn a man who had, like his associates in name if not in spirit, been executed by his own hand and had survived that death? To find such a man guilty would be redundant, a well-nigh unnecessary repetition in act of what had already transpired in idea. He had consumed himself as the apple consumed Eve, our mother and the prototype of all spiritual tarts. If Trevaskiss-Johnston manifested the cook and steward in his twoness and in his confession, Hazleton and Anderson, in the crudeness of love of money in the one and love of revenge in the other, surely figure forth the elements of the tale. The matter and spirit, apparently dehumanised as it is in these two, asserting its apparent force and strength in their actions and views of the events on the *Saladin*. They, like the others in a somewhat different way, are the gods, the spirits, of Jacob Fielding's authority and his love of it. And in them, too, we hear the authentic voice speaking, and His word is terrifying in its awful simplicity: "Vengeance is mine."

Anderson's confession was, for him, a matter of indifference to life that to him was life itself. As he had shown indifference on the ship, so he showed it now. Mutiny and confession, murder and his words were to him the same. He was the embodiment of the spirit of life through death. The self-condemnation in action proved the self-condemnation in word–he had been tried and executed on the *Saladin*; the court of law for him was a theatre where he would see himself perhaps for the first time, but without fear–how on earth can one kill a ghost? The only fear a ghost must feel is fear of birth; this Anderson was to endure. But he failed to foresee it, just as he failed to hear the authentic voice as his own closing words rang in his ears:" They told me on the night of the mutiny, that if I did not help them, they would kill me. All that I say is the truth." He ended, and a taut smile more in

29

scorn than amusement appeared on his face. His eyes were blank. The contempt he showed Sawyer and Tobe in this revealed the scorn he felt for those, he doesn't name them, who thought they could threaten the life of the spectre of security that was their god. Still grimacing, he rose, shook off the jailer's guiding hand, and returned to the only freedom he knew while his listeners pondered what they heard and saw, surfeited with food their appetites no longer required. They rose and walked into the open air, the afternoon sun low in the west. Their shadows flickered over building and alley conforming to the shapes they passed as they walked down Albermarle Street into the encroaching shadows cast by Fort George and the clock-tower which, at last, swallowed them and their shadows.

******

It wasn't until the following Tuesday, June 11, that Sawyer and Tobe once again appeared at the jail, just one month before my second day's walk took place; the day, a month later, when I walked from Chester to Indian River, from Isaac's farm to Jacob's hostelry. Jones had signified his readiness to confess. He delayed, it appeared, because he feared for his life, knowing his guilt and yet resisting the confession that would end both, apparently. In this fear he appeared to be distinctly different from his associates; they had willingly confessed, whether in the name of life or in the indifference that death shows for it. It was dusk when the High Sheriff and the Lloyd's agent appeared at the jail. They were accompanied by Johnston, the Attorney-General, who had shown interest in this last confession, owing to the prisoner's eloquent delay in delivering it. Johnston took his former seat at the head of the table, Sawyer on his left, Tobe on his right. The jailer led Jones from his cell, directly opposite the cook's, to the chair his predecessors had occupied. He sat down facing

Johnston, life-warrant in hand, after stumping across the stone floor on his wooden leg; his was a slight frame, with a tanned face and blue eyes. As he began to read, having been so ordered, his voice, marked by a noticeable Irish accent, trembled slightly. He was unnaturally pale; his hand shook like his voice. But as he continued, the trembling disappeared.

"I, George Jones, first joined the *Saladin* in Valparaiso, crew twelve in number, and two others (Captain Fielding and his son Joseph), was working my passage as a sail-maker, but acted as steward, by Captain MacKenzie's orders until after passing Cape Horn." In Jones we have the last of our double figures: Trevaskiss alias Johnston who was acting cook and then Captain, and now Jones, acting steward and sail-maker. The four make an enlightening group: cook and acting cook, steward and acting steward. As Johnston, the acting cook, became captain after Fielding dematerialised, so Jones, the acting steward, was ruler of the forecastle before Fielding became captain. It was Jones, it seemed, to whom Fielding first spoke after he had passed the Cape Horn, the Tierra del Fuego of doubt, and decided the *Saladin* was his to command. Fielding's dependence on Jones' authority in the forecastle gives mute evidence of the quality of his ascendency. Thus Jones was his man before the dream became action, just as Johnston was his first mate after it. Jones' voice, stronger now, rang in the narrow jail as he told of Fielding's first threat. " ' Now Jones, if you want to save your life, now is the time; I have spoken to the Carpenter, and I intend to be master of this ship.' " The constant knell sounds again in this: " 'if you want to save your life.' "–and Jones wanted to, needless to say. He willingly exchanged life for safety and thus fell under Fielding's Law, a man like the others he would speak to in the same cause, self-condemned to a new life that as yet was only whispered about on the darkened decks and secret meeting places of the *Saladin*. Jones shared his shipmates' hatred of MacKenzie's harshness and violence; the opportunity to in rid himself of this man presented itself through Fielding, and he took it. Jones's acquiescence only seemed a change–in actuality he replaced his actual captain with a dream-captain, just as he exchanged life for security. He found safety to be a dangerous authority, but that was later. He had vacillated; after hearing Fielding's plan, he had warned MacKenzie, only to be rejected and cursed for his pains. Like all the others tempted by gold and revenge, those twins on the *Saladin*, Jones was apparently unable to decide on a course and hold to it, to make a choice and abide by it.

The Friday night chosen for the mutiny came and went and Jones failed to appear; he had told his as yet dream-captain he hadn't known he was expected to appear. Fielding's response was, it seems to me, significant: " 'There is no use making a fool of yourself; if you go back your life is no more.' " Go back? To what? In Fielding's words, the Law of security which Jones obeyed rings out–the man who doesn't obey that Law is a fool, obedience being signified by that man's action in preserving himself! Jones capitulated; the authentic voice had spoken in Fielding's words, but neither he nor Jones heard it, or, at least, Jones joined Fielding for the second time, this time apparently without mental reservation. But did he? Jones seemed to miss witnessing most of the killings, with the exception of Johnston's beheading of the first mate while he, Jones, was at the helm. It was MacKenzie's murder in which Jones had participated, but only when Fielding, axe in hand and facing MacKenzie who had shaken off Hazleton only to have Anderson take him by the throat, had said: " 'Damn you, why don't you lay hold of him!' " And Jones complied, pinning MacKenzie's arms behind him, and being splattered by blood and brains from the axe stroke which had killed him for his pains. Jones' capitulation was his judgment, his sentence; the authentic voice was drowned, it seemed. The axe had silenced it for him and Captain Fielding drowned it astern, treading heavily on its single eye lying on deck staring at him

the moonlight that balmy night. The oath which followed on the cook's *Bible*, "to be loyal and brotherly to one another" completed the silencing, only broken now by the voice of confession in the jail which swore loyalty and brotherhood under Law by reciting his crime in public. Thus he gave final witness to the authentic voice which speaks silently in the oath on the mutinous quarterdeck, and the capitulating jail table, and my writing table in this rented room: all voices are one voice, and it sounds in silence as in articulation, mutiny or confession. Jones, the acting steward, had served his Maker well; as sail-maker his confession repaired his storm-damaged canvas to make his ship, the *Saladin* the excellent sailer she was until, like her sail-maker, she reached Harbour Island, an island albeit a floating one, in herself. The *Saladin* was Harbour Island, in the country of security where we all, prisoners, crew, sailors, lawyers, teacher and man are natives to the harbour borne. In his confession, like the others before and after, he gave up the life he had never possessed in order to possess the life that was not his to call his own. He had called it his own and so had lost it. His confession was at an end. I have heard it, am hearing it, will hear it. So be it.

Thus the dream, the plan, under the Law and witnessing the Law's power, was established through confession. The six men gave themselves to the Law in the name of an idea, an image of themselves that their crimes had painted–the models, all six, had only to pay the artist and his work was done. If MacKenzie had commissioned the painting, he was about to disappear forever, it seemed, and be replaced by Fielding, their chosen artist, MacKenzie's agent, hired to make the portraits striking likenesses, suitable for hanging in a public place. A month passed by and I arrived in the capital the night before the day of arraignment, of the public viewing of the now completed portraits. The plan, conceived en route from Valparaiso and Lunenburg and matured at Tierra del Fuego and Hubbard's was now ready to be seen for the first time.

The treasure was to be exposed to view, the food served up, and justice, paid well, and well fed, would rest comfortably, secure in his command. I stayed at the Harbour Light when I arrived on Friday night, a comfortable though somewhat small hostelry at the corner of Forman's Division and Buckingham. My landlady told me of the arraignment taking place the next day, information of which, I have no need to say now, I was already well aware. After nearly three days on the road I slept well, I must confess, in spite of the intense need I felt to see if my self-portrait of the prisoners drawn from the newspaper account of them would match the as yet unseen models for it. I felt the anxiety every artist feels when he goes on display for the first time, commissioned as I had been by MacKenzie to put his ship and crew on canvas. But MacKenzie was absent, apparently; he had disappeared at Hubbard's and I had travelled on to Halifax with Fielding and came to the Line to see, tomorrow, the result of my labours.

I awoke late the following morning, the 13th, ate the good Mrs. Painter's hearty porridge, and spent the time remaining before the arraignment walking about the chartered streets of Halifax absorbed by their geometrical patterns, losing myself in the sense of orderly security their sunlit squares provided. The buildings were for the most part freshly painted, but the colours were less bright than Lunenburg's and I found them dull by comparison. Along Forman's Division with the bright grass of the Grand Parade and the shining white St. Paul's to my right and the houses so varied in size and shape, to my left, I once again saw some evidence of civil mutiny against the wilderness as I had in the road-building of the men I met near Ingram's River. The grass of the Grand Parade was evidence of the victory, a victory I felt some doubt about sharing in whole-heartedly, however complacent the city-dwellers seemed in their citadel. I turned right at Sackville and proceeded slowly up the steep incline, once again, I noticed, following my shadow's lead–he took me to Albermarle where I turned left. He accompanied me, then, and side by side we approached two buildings about seventy-five yards ahead–the one to my right, nearest my shadow, was the Poor House, and poor it was. Windows like empty eyes looked out of its stained, mist-coloured walls. A door that undoubtedly had been red now showed the colour of an old man's toothless gums.

My eyes turned from that somewhat unnerving spectacle to the stone building on my left. Its barred windows and iron door told what its function was, making the white letters on the black sign over the door redundant. The stone was granite; in the sunlight its pepper-and -salt greyness glittered– quartz, I suppose–but the western side was shaded to near black. I stopped, momentarily, for I saw a shadowy face at one of the barred windows–all I could make out were two fiery dark eyes staring at me, an outsider, hands on the bars. His features were indistinguishable but I knew the spectre– Anderson, the avenger, at his window, enjoying the prospect of the Poor House and my spectre before him. He saw the refuge of the dispossessed and the shadow that he cast behind him in the morning sun. A chill ran through me; I felt I stood in the shadow of death, my only body now the shadow behind me, not unlike that before me behind the darkened wall and the barred window. The eyes glittered. It was only with the greatest difficulty that I broke their hold on me and escaped, turning back toward Sackville, my one shadow behind me in the cell, my other shadow to my left. Sensation left me and I became disembodied, it seemed, although my accompanying shadow showed that something must have remained standing between the sun's light and the earth over which the shadow flickered as he moved. I had indecd seen the first of the prisoners, one that, with the others, was all that remained of the *Saladin*. In his presence I had experienced a death, if transfiguration divides as a axe does, a transfiguration that recalled to my mind that other death that I felt on the mountain top at St. Margaret's head. But, clearly, this present transformation did not bring with it the sense of freedom I had felt before–the prisoner at his barred window was me, my former freedom in a new guise. The effect of the judgment I had exercised; the portrait I had painted had seemed my life and now that choosing life was revealed to me.

******

I had indeed reached the Line, MacKenzie gone and Fielding in command, the ship in his iron-handed possession, two pistols hidden beneath his table as yet undiscovered, but as intoxicating as the brandy I drank so gratefully after eating downstairs a short while ago. Spirits, spirits that even a student of morality can imbibe and find a spiritual nourishment, distilled wine–or l'*eau-de-vie*–in new bottles. Thus intoxicated I followed my shadow down Sackville Street turning left on Granville and proceeded to the Court House, a fine example of government architecture in stone, standing alone without being crowded by neighbouring refuges. The fortress of the Law, the ship of government whose commander, the Law of the Realm, had delegated his authority to men who by their word and judgment would enact the mutiny that brought shadowy criminals to life, to live anew in the Law they seemed to violate by their presence. As I entered its wide white doors in their red frame, the sensations of transfiguration I had felt at the jail intensified. It was my shadow alone who crossed the threshold and entered the courtroom already crowded by the curious, the sensation-seeker, and the idle, willing witnesses to this public exhibition of mutineers in the act of mutiny; and I was among them, unseen, my shadow elbowing his way forward to find a place of observation in the area for standing witnesses at the rear of the room.

It was a large rectangular room divided in half, appropriately enough, by a fence-like low bar looking much like a banister, without visible stairs. Behind this bar appeared a jury box on the left in front of which a table was placed for the defence lawyers. On the right was the dock. Before it the Attorney-General's table stood facing the bench where the Chief Justice and his three puisne judges would sit. My table is in the same relative position to the inn garden outside my window here as was the table for the defence to the bench; the similarity of position, in fact, is striking. The trees and rear garden wall and the sea beyond shining in the light of a setting sun occupy the same position here as the bench did there. Behind the bench was a raised dais bearing on it a throne-like golden chair where Admiral Sir Charles Adam, the naval Commander-in-Chief would sit; above him, surveying us all, young Queen Victoria's benign smile beamed regally down upon the just and the unjust, the Queen of shadows. Her portrait imaged forth the security which so grandly survives in the life that is exchanged for it, a royal Mona Lisa whose smile is not perceived to be enigmatic by those under her benign rule. She was a veritable Proserpine who gladly finished the pomegranate her lord preferred, or, perhaps more likely, a royal Diana returning the stares of the phantom dogs among whom I stood to be turned loose on those *Actaeon*s who, unseen, looked upon her smile and lusted after her in their own way.

A hush fell over the assemblage as the six prisoners entered through a door in the front wall to the right of the bench where the garden door is let into the wall that I see from my window. I was startled; they were strangers in this setting, these men, whose portraits I had painted. Their living presence, the last of the *Saladin*, gave my shadow, straining his neck to see them above the crowd in which he stood, a shuddering sense of his insubstantiality, his shadowhood. I felt him quake and strain, but remained an observer still, robbed of substance, of vital presence, only seeing through his shadowy eyes. The six were manacled and chained, these

*Actaeon*s who looked on Diana smiling down from her hanging place over the Admiral's head, just as they had seen her on the *Saladin* under Fielding's rule; he was them. Here they saw her form, and, different from the former case, they seemed transformed into justices who were confessed stags–noble animals, who would be pulled down by the men who hunted with them under Diana's auspices, Chief Justice Haliburton presiding, the master of hounds. The indictments were read charging Johnston, Jones, Hazleton and Anderson with piracy and murder–thus confessions became actions, authority became gold, as the axe fell dividing the living man from living security. This charge was the end of MacKenzie and the beginning of Fielding's regime.

I felt, phantom as I was, the division that this charge enacted as I also saw the evidence of its import on the faces of the men in the dock–they grew visibly paler, seemingly fading in the sunlight which entered through the six tall, cathedral-like windows of the room. Carr and Galloway were charged with the murder of Jacob Fielding and his son, Joseph. The confessed state was now the living state–the exchange of life for safety was witnessed but the living men, regardless of state, stood there in the dock still. Their pleas were one, at the insistence of their defence counsel and in spite of the confessions that gave them life and cut them off. "'Not guilty!'" Johnston spoke for them all, their captain still. Thus they asserted their innocence, but the irony behind the plea was not because of their confessed guilt but because in it once again the authentic voice spoke. This voice gave witness to their being charged for deeds for which judgment and execution had already been carried out as it was on the decks of the *Saladin*–a clear case of double jeopardy! Their guilt only made their crime, their dream, into an actuality, just as their axes had. And now their common plea asserted the unreality of their dream of security whether by axe or confession, action or word–once that dream was made real the living man, no dream, I am assured, would disappear, pulled down by mutinous phantom dogs hungering after justice. Not guilty–not guilty of exchanging life for safety because such exchange cannot be made. Life is not a commodity for exchange, apparently, even if Fielding and his followers tried to make it so. Not guilty! And so the sounds of arraignment ended drowned in the noise of shuffling feet as my shadow, wearied by the strain, tired from the press he had stood in for so long, and puzzled by the plea, perhaps, made his way to the Harbour Light. In the late afternoon sunlight as I flickered against the walls of buildings, alleys and streets bound by his movements but free to find my being in the form and order of the constructs of refuge we call a city. This is our confession of a crime we didn't commit in order to see before our eyes evidence to prove the guilt we feel–guilt, one sees, can be a sign of life. It gives voice, if we can only hear it, to the life that we attempt to exchange for security and so seek to turn life itself into a transferable commodity. My God! We are possessed!

The five days until Thursday, the 18th, passed quickly. Not unexpectedly, I do not recall them; it was my shadow that walked and talked, ate and slept through them waiting the concluding word at the trial. My shadow rose early on Thursday morning, observed his customary ritual and arrived in the Court Room an hour before the trial was to commence. I was still an accessory after the fact, a *corpus delicti* that could so strangely resist exorcism even in such surroundings, not unlike the six that appeared in the dock paired together by iron handcuffs. Although it was to be the trial of the four, excepting the cook and steward who were charged under a separate indictment, all six were present. Those to be tried and those not to be tried chained together in the same dock. My shadow and I presented a similar condition. Shortly after the prisoners, the jury took their benches on the left, followed by the defence attorneys. The morning sun shone brightly into the east windows and into the eyes of the jury; they could not see the dock or the men in it except as shadows. The sunlight also hid from them the Attorney-General, William Johnston, who took his seat below his namesake in the dock as the Chief Justice entered. The Honourable Brenton Haliburton was a pale man in his early fifties, partly ruddy-cheeked with watery blue eyes that seemed to belie their piercing glance. He was accompanied by three puisne judges, in wig and robe as was their chief; all took their seats, the Honourable Blowers Bliss and the Honourable William Hill to the Chief Justice's left and the Honourable T. C. Haliburton to his right. The justly famed Sam Slick would find sharp bargaining aplenty in this day's work.

The attorneys and the audience were eagerly awaiting the trial; even the prisoners also, who looked across at the gold-encrusted jury bedecked by the sunlight, so many golden Mexican dollars filling the box to the brim. The prisoners before the Chief Justice were facing themselves; he would sentence them in the voice which had sentenced them on the decks of the *Saladin* seen and so heard in their actions, now heard again in his words. That, it seems, was their prison, their Cape Horn, the irremediable connection. The last to enter was Admiral Sir Charles Adam, who took his seat behind and above the Chief Justice. His name was not inappropriate for the presiding figure in the room, surveying as he did the Eden of the Law from a position beyond it and below the smiling image of the Queen he served, an imperial Eve and her loyal Adam. Resplendent in his naval uniform with its golden epaulettes and stripes, buttons and decorations, the dark blue a striking setting for the glitter enhanced by the morning sun. He looked the embodiment of sea and sun, elemental and eternal, sitting above and apart from the red robes of judgment seated below him, red as the blood they sought. And there also was their Queen smiling on above them, blessing them, apparently, in their innocent pursuit of this stag whose life, if that was what I may call it, was the object of the hunt. The taking of this life that they had joined so willingly together to effect through the dignity of mutiny made Law.

The Attorney-General rose to address the Court and jury. His was the imposing figure I have already described in the confession scene in the jail. He was a staunch Baptist whose cold exercise of reason and clarity of judgment made me shiver while my shadow warmed to his opening words. The case, it seemed, was unusual–imagine, redundancy as unusual; the repetition of the exchange which the six had made in the exchange they were about to see and hear transpire before their eyes–and so, apparently was the constitution of the court. It was a trial of mixed commission, it seemed–how ironic legal jargon can sound–since offences committed beyond the limits of the realm are not under the jurisdiction of ordinary courts of law. In other words, the court had no jurisdiction! Like the exchange that can not be made, the court could not pass judgment on its prisoners! There is the voice again, speaking out, but, apparently, not for long. Johnston continued by citing precedents, first one from Henry the Eighth's reign that permitted such offences to be tried according to the forms of Common Law Courts. The Henry, so well known for his ability to manipulate jurisdiction, one recalls, as Sir Thomas More might as well; Sir Thomas refused to participate in his sovereign's Reformation and so gained the life King Henry tried to deny him, clearly a marriage of convenience. Quite a precedent in this present case! Another was cited from William the Third's reign that extended this power to the Colonies– our court was thus legally granted jurisdiction. Already one sees in this the beginnings of exchange, or the first glimpse of Diana's image arising, as it did and does, before my eyes. But perhaps unseen by the others in the court, their eyes being dazzled by *Apollo*'s rays shining through the windows and filling the room with his light.

In exchange for safety, for jurisdiction, then, the Attorney-General had confined himself already, and the court was duly constituted in thus blindly accepting his precedents, mutinous in intent as they clearly were. He continued, having thus confined himself, and rounded Cape Horn in his subsequent description of what constituted the burden of proof— burden indeed! If it could be shown that there had been a union and a combination among all the prisoners, and that the crimes charged were indeed committed, the jury's verdict must be given accordingly. Where the citing of precedents began, the burden of proof continued to bring about the exchange: the burden, surprisingly enough, was two-fold according to Johnston: first, the existence of a unity among the six prisoners, and, then, second, that the crimes had actually been committed. Were the six one? Clearly they were in their willingness to exchange life for security on the *Saladin* but their unity was not confined to the now ghostly ship! It rose to engulf the court itself and its voice was heard in Johnston's words. My God, I saw then as I see now that unity, all-encompassing, which the Attorney-General used as part of the proof of guilt! The other part was the actuality of the crime— and once again the unity I am asserting clarified itself. There was a crime, and it was being perpetrated in the court, self-crowned with jurisdiction. Before it in the dock stood the self-declared *corpus delicti*, the confessed that in doing so had created their guilt in order to save themselves! In *them* I see the court before which they stood on trial for confessing to acting on an exchange that cannot be made. It should be no surprise to me, then, when the Attorney-General continued his account of the Country Harbour events and Captain Cunningham's discoveries on board the wrecked ship. But his major assertion was a striking example of the exchange he sought to make rising to action in his words. He returned to the jail he had visited five days before and told the court of the confessions the six had submitted; as I see it now, the plot was now planted, growing and ripening to maturity. The case would be put to the jury chiefly on those confessions.

What could the jury do now? What was their function? They had none since the prisoners had clearly conspired with the court; those twelve good men and true in their legal function evaporated before my eyes. The prisoners, looking across the court, saw the gold-bedecked, sun-adorned jury, their prize, not lost to the government as they had thought, but rediscovered in the men they faced. The jury, eyes sun-dimmed, saw themselves in irons awaiting judgment. Their legal function, it seemed, was to evaporate like the dim shapes before them which they could hardly see–images one of the other, mirrored there, Narcissus-like. And they were turning imperceptibly into the plant that grew before them, forced to bloom unnaturally by the Attorney-General's guano-like words as he proceeded with the narrative of confession.

After the *Saladin* rounded Cape Horn, Fielding proposed to Jones that they rise against the officers and take the vessel and cargo. These two then enlisted three others, apparently, and the plot gradually ripened. The prisoners were now MacKenzie, Byerby and the still loyal members of the crew in my vision. The maturing plot transpiring before my eyes fused the *Saladin* and the court, and I felt us round Tierra del Fuego and head north-east toward the Line only far ahead now in imaginary nautical miles, not in present time. The *Saladin's* gold was the exchange Johnston sought, one sees, his plant flowering before his eyes as his words flowed on. My shadow among shadows saw only justice being done; so be it. After all, they were attempting to give substance to the visible justice they sought, seen not only in their plot but also in my perception of their role. And the plot gradually ripened, to repeat the Attorney-General's words. And the central question remains; do I have the authority, the control to withhold judgment? In what way does my telling of it condemn and exonerate me at the same time? Is there such a thing as reasonable culpability? I, perhaps, shall come to see.

Johnston's words will help, it seems, as they flowed on

telling of his, of Fielding's, *modus operandi*: by holding communication with each man separately, and threatening each that others would aid him if they did not, he urged on his–of all words–diabolical work; the time arrived for action! Shades of the prison house close upon the Attorney-General and those separate confessions, holding communication with each man separately, as he, in themselves, held council and decided to confess. And so, standing in the dock before the court, the time for action had indeed arrived. As Johnston's account of the murder of the first mate continued, based as it was on the confessions, the axe is his words, the victim the prisoners. He brought it down heavily upon them, throwing them overboard with mutinous strength. They were in one foul conspiracy and all were equally criminal in the eyes of the Law; my eyes were opened in that–the eyes of the Law were my eyes. What they saw was the one foul conspiracy before me. The authentic Law by which we live was seen through this shadowy outward and visible sign, the trial, to create a substantial inward and spiritual grace–this was and is the only cargo of value, and the *Saladin* carried it for me, to me, in me. The Attorney-General's voice continued; he axed the first mate, the Carpenter, and now, MacKenzie himself. The Carpenter's crying "murder" as he floated astern brought the Captain on deck. Johnston's description of this is telling, it seems to me: the cry "murder" was made use of with fiendish ingenuity. It was converted into a means of aiding their bloody purposes, since it was the cry that brought MacKenzie to his quarterdeck, or to his dock in the court. The confessions cried "murder" as the confessors floated away and those confessions were clearly used, converted, into a means of aiding the court's bloody work. Johnston used the view that the desire for security is evil, being fiendishly ingenious as he said. Fiendish indeed! Johnston had condemned the court in which he was a prosecutor in the same words in which he exonerated it. Is fiendish a proper word to describe his ingenuity? The *Saladin* was then taken charge of by Fielding, not dead, but heard in the Attorney-General's words as the trial continued.

The cook and the steward appeared on deck the next morning. Fielding told them that their lives were given them on conditions–on conditions! How was Johnston's preferred confession to the prisoners different from Fielding's to cook and steward? Were not the prisoners being offered safety in exchange for life? Johnston was the cook-legitimate and the Chief Justice was the high steward, his stewardship the stewardship of the Law under the smiling sovereign hanging over his head. They were given their lives on conditions, the cook and steward; the conditions were their acquiescence in giving their lives to the proposition that the exchange of life for safety is legitimate. Johnston's and Fielding's similarity in their giving of life on condition, therefore, is further illuminated, perhaps, by observing that the cook and the steward quickly accepted Fielding's conditions, just as they were the first to offer their confessions to Johnston. In addition, Carr and Galloway were tried separately from the others for their crimes, although they appeared in the dock with their shipmates when the other four were tried. The common goal, the common treasure, sought by everyone in the courtroom was imaged forth in these two men, separate and united in dock as in service yet set apart. Yes, united but set apart, tried separately, they lived on to serve Fielding's Law too. They killed him; they killed his son–now here's the authentic voice, the Law of exchange in action still. The man who devotes himself to establishing the reality of his desire to exchange life for safety dies, as the food he eats dies–he consumes himself in the name of security and reveals the Law of exchange. In this present case, he very simply dies, thrown overboard, creator and creature, father and son.

And what of Johnston and his case? In the death of the father and son at the hands of cook and steward he said that there never was a more striking instance of retributive justice overtaking the guilty; cooks and stewards are, to the Attorney-General, agents of justice! The *Saladin's* decks, bloodstained as they were, and containing below them, the gold, the treasure, was the security all aboard her sought. The *Saladin*'s deck is a court of Law in Johnston's eyes; the exchange is effected–*consummatum est*–the Attorney-General had, in this, not only successfully rounded Cape Horn and Tierra del Fuego, but he was well on his way to the Line. And he continued, mutineer-legitimate that he was. Fielding and his son were made to share the fate of those men whom he had mercilessly sent to an untimely grave, but the cook and steward had not, as yet, acted but had only joined him in his devotion. The interval was filled with events that can be briefly reviewed in further illustration of this–dare I call it case? Following the oath of brotherhood which united cook and steward with Fielding and the others, the consequences underlying the conditions which gave them life, in the Attorney-General's words as well as Fielding's, began to show themselves in two striking forms. First was the discovery of the two horse-pistols hidden, of all places, under the cabin table! As Hazleton is reported to have said at the time, " 'this means something,' " as he faced, pistols in hand, his captain. The threat in this, embodied for them in him, told them their exchange had never taken place at all. As they threatened the authentic voice, so they felt threatened by it–an example of the Law of exchange in its simplest form, it seems to me, made visible, at last, in the horse-pistols under the cabin table. And under the Attorney-General's table a similar threat was discovered, the horse-pistols of guiltlessness, of innocence most easily seen in this unity with the mutineers. To a prosecutor in such a case, innocence is as a death. And as he spoke he looked at two men in the dock in particular: Johnston now alias Trevaskiss, and Jones, acting cook and acting steward; exchange, I see, is double-barrelled. The acting cook and acting steward who, accepting their confessions as valid evidence for unachieved exchange, accused them before the bar of the Queen's justice under her smiling eyes. To act can be a trial.

If the first sign of consequences was the discovery of the pistols, the second was Anderson's open betrayal of Fielding's plot against his sworn brothers. The pistols first showed the consequences, and Anderson's revelation was the powder and ball that, discharged, apparently destroyed the father and son. Safety betrayed betrays itself in taking a death-like form. All that remained was that cook and steward kill the father and son, the agents of what Johnston had called a striking instance of retributive justice, for heaven's sake! The advocate of the illusion of exchange was, to all appearances, dead and gone. Johnston was the newly discovered commander; the captain is dead, long live the captain! Here we see continuity, may I even call it legitimate life, looming up in a vision in which the agents drift mistily before our eyes while their actions speak in the authentic voice, the unexchangeable. Once again I see two captains with one name before us–the court bound them together, a court which was a prison, a cave-like refuge exposed when the uprooted tree of knowledge leaves a pocket in the earth, its fruit scattered around it on the ground. The Attorney-General's voice sounded stronger now as he concluded. If all these facts were true which he had revealed, one tenth of what these men did would constitute the crime of piracy–a tithe, a tithe for the landlord's sustenance or the parson's support. Anderson, he continued, told the whole truth–revenge, and betrayal– only the others slanted their tales in their own favour. The soul shudders at the scene disclosed by these unhappy men, and I'm quoting Johnston's words here, that most unhappy man. His concluding sentence carries its own treasured reward within it. Citing the *Saladin's* case generally, he stated that British Commerce, growing as it had been, needed the protection of the Law. It is that protection alone which had given security to the mariner, and guarded the interests of the whole civilised world. The Attorney-

eral's gold was apparently safely in his hands. The words of the shadowy prosecutor rang in the ears of the now-shadowy accused: their mutual conspiracy established the legitimacy of the exchange they coveted, sought, and apparently found. The Attorney-General had been, it seems, an efficient gardener. The seed he planted had flowered and now bore fruit– the golden apples were within his reach, golden apples whose illusory if tempting beauty was only equalled by their inability to satisfy the appetite of the one who hungered after them. Johnston's case for the Crown was closed, his mutiny apparently successful, his victims cut down by the axe-legitimate.

The defense at first declined to address the court, so loath were they, apparently, to put into question the security so ingeniously established by the Attorney-General's mutiny-legitimate, so absolute seemed the reality of the exchange. But the prisoners apparently desired that all that could be said should be said in defence not only of themselves but also of the Attorney-General. Johnston, it seemed, wished to make a statement. He referred to his original plea of not guilty given at the arraignment–how strange it sounded now–and, in justice to his feelings and in reconciliation of his awakened and guilty conscience, he now wished to change his plea to guilty! Here I see a living, substantial, waking conscience speaking in the dock before his embodied namesake whose establishment of guilt had brought the conscience to wakefulness. As a result it would see its continued life, exchanged at the expense of life itself–or so it seemed to me in the court. Johnston continued. He placed his life in the hands of the court. My God, here is the fear, the life as possession, apparently, being passed, like an object, into the willing hands of the mutineer-legitimate who had already taken it! And what was Johnston's continued plea, his defense? It had been Fielding's powers of persuasion, the plausible reasoning and persuasiveness of that fiend in human shape! How plausible is Johnston's reasoning, here, an ironic echo of his name-sake's reasoning. The

Genprisoner defends the words of his prosecutor in the name of attempting to appear less guilty! He finished his statement at last, having referred to his comrades as witnesses to his truth, and thanked the court for the humane treatment he had received while he was imprisoned. His guilt was now his life; a prison cell was his home, and gallows his means to life, that trcc of knowledge from whose single branch hangs the single fruit of such a plant.

George Young, a dignified and handsome man, an author as well as a lawyer, rose and addressed the court on behalf of himself and Lawrence Doyle, attorneys for the defence, in matters of extenuation. In my eyes, this defence was for the benefit of the court and was addressed to the prisoners whose living presence judged their judges. The defence adduced the prosecution and was itself part of the court. Young said there was no doubt but that all the prisoners at the bar were the victims of that wretch who had been truly described as a fiend in human shape. How like the creation of Adam—though here tempting words replace breath and ears replace our progenitor's nostrils–the creation of life! And the words of the attorney for the defence sound in my ears too, but hardly to tempt me, or perhaps to do just that. Yes, to tempt me to recognise in this the authentic voice whispering to inform us of the life revealed in the difference between the man, Fielding or Johnston, the living man, and he who devoted his life to the security he might find in exchange for it. This might well tempt the Attorney-General, too, bringing before his unwilling eyes the innocence standing before him whispering in his ear of the crimes he perpetrated. Young's defence rested further on Fielding's consummate art by which he called forth the prisoner's cupidity and alarmcd their fears. He told them the other watch was ready if they refused, the other watch, standing in the dock; the other watch standing by to take over control of the ship if safety became danger. The defence then called the court's attention, in summation, to what it saw as a central issue in the case; the prisoners were drawn into crime by the force of circumstance! Not men but circumstances are the creators of action, of life! The defence, I see, was finally pleading the prosecution's case as a defence for the men it would apparently condemn.

The Chief Justice's charge to the jury which followed this–could it still be a jury?–this defensive prosecution revealed the master of hounds, the high steward. Safe at last, he admonished a jury robbed of its function by what appeared to be an ironic *fait accompli*. That shadowy jury was told it ought not to allow any feeling of compassion to interfere with the strict course of justice, or to efface impressions which advocates were apt to make. How might functionless shadows have feelings at all, let alone compassion, or, how might a shadow interfere in anything, let alone justice! The Chief Justice's words were addressed to living men with feelings and, by their very existence, did interfere with the strict course of justice. But the court reduced these living men to shadows that, looking at the dock opposite, only saw themselves and the guilt of being living men who had acted in the cause of justice. The high steward continued: as men of sense, then, the jury would ask, was it reasonable, if not influenced by criminal motives, that these men could, under such circumstances, have been compelled to shed the blood of those men they might so easily have warned of their danger for self-defence? Clearly the Chief Justice had self-defence in mind here, if not influenced by criminal motives, didn't he? The personification of safety, this personification of safety, I say, recommends bloodshed for self-defence. The innocence of this man is unlimited, and his words sound it forth as his intentions betray him; his innocence is about to unleash the shadowy hounds whose prey is the *Actaeon* in the dock all beneath our Queen's, Diana's, graven image.

He closed his charge with telling words. While he found cases of criminal nature to be painful to courts and juries, he had never known one less perplexing, less trying to the feelings than the present one. His simplicity is overwhelming, isn't it? No doubt in *his* mind! There was apparently no case, since cases would seem to imply some degree of conflict, of question, and here there was none. No case, no jurisdiction, no court, no Chief Justice, no jury, no defence and, last but not least, no crime but his own! There's security for you: safety in murder, in piracy, in acting or speaking in the interests of exchanging life for security in the court as on the *Saladin*. Safety in non-existence, I see, but how does one achieve this desirable condition? By killing, that's how!–by taking, whether by word or deed, the life in the name of safety by the instrument of exchange, whether it takes the form of uniting axes or dividing maul, dividing judgment or uniting rope. "Mariners," the Chief Justice concluded, "are in an especial manner bound to protect the life of the master with whom they sail. The peace of society requires that crime should be punished." The ghostly jury returned in fifteen minutes with the court's verdict–Guilty. Safe at last weren't they? The substantiated shadows filed from the dock, bench, jury-box and tables from which the excellent repast had been successfully prepared and served, eaten and digested by those shadows, the audience not excepted–my shadow among them. I followed, feeling a death-bearing wind blowing within me as I returned with him on his right hand flickering over the objects he passed in the pale afternoon sun; a cloud, it seemed, could easily consign me to non-existence. But no cloud came and I thoroughly enjoyed Mrs. Painter's generous supper that my shadow found unpalatable, even threatening, seemingly condemning him to eat when he was already filled to capacity by the legitimate food he was served at the court.

******

The following morning we arose early. I ate the

fast that my shadow refused, complaining of lack of appetite which neither Mrs. Painter nor I believed; he was, of course, planning to eat elsewhere, namely, at "The Sign of the Trap," also known as the Queen's Arms. We therefore proceeded with all due speed to the court once more to watch the trial of cook and steward; whether they were on the bench or in the dock remained to be seen. The courtroom filled with shadows as on the previous day, officials as well as watchers, my shadow among those seated at the bar that separated one watch from the other. There were to be two trials that day; one for the murder of Fielding and the other for the murder of his son. What has been one yesterday was divided into two today; yesterday's instrument the axe of safety, today's the maul of life. I looked forward to an exchange myself in this. It was soon in evidence as the proceedings opened in due course.

It began with an echo from yesterday's trial. The defence asked the court to permit the four tried yesterday to change their former plea of not guilty, as regarded the murder of Fielding, to plead guilty now. Exchange indeed! The four now saw themselves as guilty of a crime three of them had not committed, much like their prosecutor and Chief Justice. They apparently saw themselves as not guilty of a crime they had palpably committed in their well-nigh tyrannical devotion and the validity of the exchange that gave it life at the expense of life itself. The four prisoners, those judges, had condemned the court to innocence; the evidence of their plea was unassailable proof of this and I am the star witness for the prosecution, an attorney-at-large whose case against the court is nearly won in this. The new plea was accepted; only the cook and steward, therefore, remained to be tried. The Attorney-General, fresh from the previous day's victorious mutiny-legitimate, rose to address the court charging the cook and steward with the murder of Captain Fielding. Remember that the cook and steward had thrown him overboard, just as Johnston had gained command of the trial by apparently sucbreakcessfully condemning the other prisoners, the MacKenzie of life in exchange for the Fielding of safety. These assembled notaries of self-preservation were once again indulging themselves in establishing guilt for what they saw as a non-existent crime. The Attorney-General proceeded to describe this crime. The cook's and the steward's case, it seemed, was less flagrant than that presented yesterday. Fielding, in order to carry out his diabolical designs–a devil's if not a devilishly ingenious advocate was Johnston–into execution in obtaining possession of the *Saladin* must needs kill her captain and overpower the crew. Four down and two to go must have been Johnston's thought at this moment, unaware, perhaps, of his self-portrait resembling more and more closely a portrait of the so-called dead Fielding.

After the captain and part of the crew was gone, the prisoners now on trial remained to be disposed of. Having come under Fielding's command, the cook and steward found themselves treated differently from the other prisoners. Fielding's hiding of the horse-pistols caused suspicions to arise. They were brought into the open through an accusation of treachery when Anderson betrayed Fielding's plot to kill his sworn brothers, among them, of course, the cook and steward. Where is Johnston now? Isn't his plot clearly in evidence? The plot was not only contrived against the lives of cook and steward but would be, perhaps, of more far-reaching consequences. And how did he bring their guilt forward? He pointed out their concurrence in the false statements made by the others to Cunningham and later to their examiners; for example, like the others, they made statements to the effect that Fielding had died in Valparaiso before the *Saladin* sailed. False indeed, since he faced them there giving voice to their accusation–Captain Johnston, the third but not last Captain of the *Saladin*. According to Johnston their false statements pointed toward their guilt, and then he proceeded to describe Fielding further. Guilty as the man unquestionably was, his bloodstained soul ushered by violence into the presence of the Great Judge of the Universe, and notwithstanding his crimes, he was still within the protection of the Law. Johnston clearly pleads for Fielding's safety under Law–retributive justice he called it the day before when he described the cook's and steward's killing Fielding, seeing them as agents of justice– here he is clearly pleading his own defence. He, too, was still within the protection of the Law like Fielding; if so, the cook and the steward in the dock were not the agents of justice he had seen them as yesterday. They were guilty murderers–a telling exchange: one-time agents of justice now become killers to be condemned under the Law for which they formerly acted as agents. Johnston was clearly attempting to show security as culpable in the court where its innocence was the house rule. Peculiar predicament for a prosecutor; but then, prosecution has its dangers, I find. This closed the case for the Crown. Johnston, the defender of safety, had, in palpably attacking it in the persons of the cook and steward, exchanged safety for life. His prosecution was ironically transformed into a brilliant defence. The Law's protection that he claimed for Fielding, in spite of his crimes and the vision of his bloody soul, he innocently claimed for himself.

James B. Uniacke, a huge man of rugged physique and rocky features, rose to speak in defence of the cook and steward. His evident pride and self-possession sounded in his deep, powerful voice, an appropriate configuration of the safety Johnston's words had accused of culpability. Safety had a new advocate in him who began by saying it was impossible to conceal the responsibility he felt in the present occasion. He claimed, as his associate Young had the day before, that the circumstances connected with Fielding's death were such as would legally justify the act in the eyes of a humane British jury. There's security for you! Uniacke–an engaging name in itself, I find, suggesting as it does a certain oneness–the defence attorney uses safety as if it were Law. What had demned the former four was now cited as an unwritten law which would defend the cook and steward against the inroads of the murderous arguments of a prosecutor who, in spite of his crimes, still enjoyed the protection of the Law he had apparently violated. The golden apple of victory he had enjoyed in yesterday's trial was taken from him.

But Uniacke's defence was prosecution for Johnston. The cook and the steward with Uniacke's eloquent defence would throw Captain Johnston overboard and his case with him. In all criminal cases the Law requires free agency, and sanctions deeds of violence necessary for self-preservation! He then showed that in the murder of–Fielding was the name he used, but Johnston seems as just–in the murder of Fielding they were involuntarily acting, and were activated by motives of self-preservation. Last but not least, Uniacke claimed they had no alternative! The apparently dead Fielding speaks on in this in the defence of his would-be murderers. Having robbed his clients of the power of choice in their defence, he now proceeded to proclaim their innocence! After the deed was done, the cook and the steward were morally innocent of his death–what on earth happened to the crime? Clearly it had disappeared through the innocence of the defence. The exoneration of cook and steward makes murder innocent; the prosecutor's legal death in losing the condemnation he sought is, therefore, no death at all, but a source of life to him; he kills to save, and, of course, saves to kill. The cook and the steward, Uniacke continued, were intimidated by superior physical force; fear drove them. But what of the defence attorney? In proving their innocence in this fashion wasn't he also robbing them of their life, their power of choice, their very being? Such a defence was prosecution, a prosecution not unlike Johnston's of yesterday–and what if a man who seeks security and finds fear is like a lunatic, an idiot or a monomaniac? Desiring safety above life itself; isn't this murder, perhaps? Johnston's prosecution was the cook's and ard's only defence; now Uniacke's eloquent defence prosecuted the case and so condemned them to innocence, a guilt of which they were entirely innocent.

The defence attorney's closing remarks make a suitable summary of his prosecution of cook and steward, granting them as it eventually did, the killing safety of spectrehood. Uniacke proceeded thus: he said that it was in doubt with some whether, in any case, life should be taken. If it was wrong to inflict capital punishment in crimes of the deepest dye–the metaphor is significant–how much more would it be so in the present case, where so many mitigating circumstances were to be taken into consideration. Oh, the pity of it, the pity of it–mitigating circumstances, indeed! What Uniacke called mitigating circumstances were, of course, the cook and steward, Carr and Galloway, living men whose only safety was that they didn't seek it; but it was being handed to them as, of all things, a defence. Uniacke's defence was as much a threat to them as was the prosecutor's attack a life-giving defence.

The Chief Justice addressed a jury whose former ghostliness was now seen to be only apparent as they looked into the dock and saw living men condemned to innocence as they themselves were. The Chief Justice warned them that the case had been presented as if Fielding had not been under the protection of the Law. But he said, with an irony that cannot be overlooked even when it is heard in the voice of that master of the hounds, no man could be placed in such a situation. Fielding was as much under the protection of the Law as the most innocent man living–and who was more innocent than the high steward who said this, or his acting cooks, Johnston and Uniacke? He concluded by saying that according to the confessions of the prisoners he thought the jury were bound to find them guilty–a master of hounds still, unleashing his phantoms to pull down the ghostly animals who stood still in the dock. The jury, duly admonished, retired for a short time and returned to their places quietly. They folconstewlowed the spirit of the Chief Justice's orders, if not the letter: the verdict was not guilty. Carr wept openly when he heard this, but over the steward's face passed a momentary fleeting smile; the cook wept for his lost guilt, but the steward smiled in his innocence. The cook and steward had successfully thrown the prosecution and Chief Justice overboard with the help of a defence which robbed them of their life as it offered them, in exchange for life, security.

After a brief recess, during which time the court, jury, lawyers and prisoners withdrew, my substantial shadow and the audience remained in their places. The day before they had seen the desire for safety made a crime; today it was not made a crime, but a form of Law. As a crime it made the guilt for which four men would be punished, but as a form of Law it made the innocence for which two men would be released without punishment. One day's trial shadows forth another–Johnston, Jones, Hazleton and Anderson are the doubled shadows of Carr and Galloway–as if the cook and steward stood beneath two suns. One trial for the four; two trials for the two–two is one by the magic of legal mathematics, at least.

The court reconvened, constituted as it was earlier in the day. The Attorney-General, resurrected, apparently, by this resurrected court and a new opportunity to find those innocent of the death of the father guilty of the death of the son. How could one kill the son without killing the father–or how could one kill the son if he were innocent of the father's death? The prosecutor's case, if he had one, was, in the son's case, apparently, to deny the life united in the father and son, two forms of a single force. The cook and steward, found innocent of Fielding's death (but hardly of Johnston's) were to be found guilty of his son's death if the prosecution were effective. In wild abandon, Johnston was adopting a view that even to a greater degree than in yesterday's trial attacked safety itself, apparently. In dividing father and son by determining the guilt or innocence of the cook and steward in their deaths,

and in death they are seen to be one as they are in life. The golden apple was, it seems, inaccessible; and he, would-be captain of the court and *Saladin*, lost his ship and case; Harbour Island revealed its hidden reef, but Johnston didn't see it, drunk as he was with the l'*eau-de-vie* of security. He stated in addressing the court that he felt it unnecessary to go into a detail of the whole matter connected with the scenes that had taken place on board the *Saladin*. The events on the *Saladin* thus evaporate, unnecessary, irrelevant and immaterial; the Attorney-General's words embody legitimate safety before our eyes, life thus fully exchanged for safety and life itself apparently dismissed as immaterial!

The prosecutor was, beyond a shadow of a doubt, a pillar of the court he served, supporting it as Atlas supports the World on his shoulders, feet planted securely in the Garden where the trees bear golden apples, the Garden of the Hesperides, but Atlas cannot touch the apples he covets. His burden is too great, the burden of proof! He continued by describing the cook's and the steward's fears for their safety as the motive for the killing of Fielding of which they were exonerated. They had been required by the others to act in their capacity of cook and steward, and they had done so till the moment when the crime was committed of which they stood charged. Whatever apprehensions they may have entertained that induced them to throw the father overboard could not, he said, be urged as a palliation with regard to the deliberate destruction of the son. That they thought the boy might in future appear against them as a witness could neither justify nor lessen the heinous nature of the crime of which they stood charged. The only testimony that would be produced against them was their own confession. The prosecutor sees the cook and steward as fearful, and, I think, I agree. They had good reason to fear as they saw the safety they sought become a threat to their existence; Fielding and his pistols, or Johnston and his legal security. Their confessions were to be the only testimony, confessions that were offered in the name of witnessing to the actuality of the crime they committed. Their innocence in this was clear, just as Johnston's was. All three were conspiring to make the act, the confession, the guilt an actuality and the court was there, as before, to approve their action. But the prosecutor chose his words carefully, making his case against them. Finally it seems as if it had no bearing in the events on the *Saladin*, on the men themselves, but only on the confessions, thus openly revealing, unaware, his own confession of guilty participation in this attempt to throw innocence overboard, having previously gone over the side himself. Johnston's attempt to overthrow innocence, to reveal safety as an absolute and as such a threat to life has its irony because, as in the previous trial that day, although his case was attacking the cook and steward for their desire to survive, he also attacked the desire to survive itself. And so, of course, he became the blind advocate of life itself, the authentic voice. The case for the Crown was closed. Their ghostly presences awaited their defence.

James Uniacke, enheartened by his previous victory, rose to address the court. He said that notwithstanding what had fallen from the bench in the charge to the jury on the former trial, he should still entertain his own view of the Law. There might be modern constructions of the Criminal Law which courts were slow to recognise. Here we see the wily defender taking the Law into his own hands for safety's sake and the sake of Carr and Galloway–a modern construction indeed! If the prosecutor had successfully defended safety in condemning the men who had acted in accordance with it, the defence counsel would successfully prosecute such a defence and so prove the men innocent–the men, of course, including not only the cook and steward but also the Attorney-General. The Law of survival, the prosecutor claimed, was not a mitigating circumstance. Uniacke took a different view in the name of his own survival and that of the Law he served. He reasoned that just as threats are not allowable in obtaining confessions, so threats to the cook's and the steward's lives were not allowable in attempting to prove them guilty. When they performed an unwilling part at the command of the pirates, who had previously doomed to death the father and son, the guilt, it seemed, lay in the threatener, not in the threatened! Just as threat invalidates confession, so fear invalidates guilt. Fear is the creation of innocence, it seems, and so the desire for safety is, being the creator of fear in the first place, also innocent!

Uniacke's plea is the legal principle he voiced, exemplifying as it does the desire to survive and the fear such desire creates, but, most noteworthy of all, reveals the man's innocence when we consider his intention. He intended to show the cook's and the steward's helplessness, their inability to do anything other than what they did: they killed Fielding and his son. Uniacke, therefore, was defending his clients by denying their existence, denying their part in their actions. By thus condemning them to death he proved their innocence and the validity of the Law of Survival for himself and the court, shadows all applauding their own death, echoing the steward's momentary smile as he heard himself declared innocent of Fielding's death. They were in a position that left them no choice in committing the fearful deed, for their own lives were in jeopardy. Thus Carr and Galloway do not exist for Uniacke in this any more than they had for Johnston when he found the details of events on the *Saladin* to be unnecessary and immaterial. Like his clients, Uniacke then stated that the two acts, that of destroying the father and the son, were in reality one, and they were compelled to perform them to save themselves. I note that he puts father and son together in this in order to prove the innocence of their murderers. Overboard he went, and his clients with him, not to mention the court itself–innocent enough, it seems to me. As before he quoted precedents to show the Law's sanction of violence for self-preservation–as if he needed to under such circumstances–

and how fear compelled men to perform acts of desperation! Fear, it seems, was the living, commanding force in men's actions, leaving the men themselves to slavery under the fear that controlled them. Men, therefore, were created by fear and thus were the creatures of their own fear. A revealing view in the voice of a would-be defence attorney–defence be damned! Thus we hear the condemnation of life itself, thus relegated to impotence and servitude in the name of survival, of innocence. The case for the defence closed on this innocent note. What a trial it had been, from beginning, if it had one, to end, if it does. I have reached the Line with the court by means of it and the *Saladin*.

As before, the Chief Justice charged the jury, but not in the same terms. In the present instance, he found, the appeal made by the prisoner's counsel was in more legitimate order than in the former trial; indeed it was, since Uniacke had apparently thrown innocence over the side. Legitimate ordering made prosecution into defence and defence into prosecution in the name of security. The Chief Justice saw the legitimacy of the Law of Survival thus tacitly condemning his prosecutor and acquitting his defence. But the Chief Justice's short address had not ended. He closed by stating that if the circumstances were such that they were compelled to do the act, the Law would hold them guiltless. But was this the case? He thought not. He read parts of the confessions showing that such compulsion was lacking which the Law could recognise as justification. In his view the jury should find the prisoners guilty. The Chief Justice reveals in this admonition a divided view of the case before him. First, he cited the validity of Uniacke's plea that the Law of Survival be accepted as the Law of the Realm; and, second, he cited the validity of the Law under which Carr and Galloway should be condemned as the violators of the Law of safety. Here are both safety and life held up as objects before the court and the Chief Justice's non-choice is clearly choice itself. The two prisoners and the two objects–or life and safety. If safety was his object then life must be exchanged for it; condemnation is salvation, or, more plainly, perhaps, guilt is innocence.

The Chief Justice's apparent twoness of view is the authentic voice speaking through a legal mask. No wonder the graven image above him smiled so benignly. He had chosen; he chose the object before the man. The jury retired and returned two hours later. Their choice was more difficult than the Chief Justice's: they had to rule on the Law of Survival, and once more they obeyed the Chief Justice's mandate in spirit if not in letter. The cook and steward were not guilty, they said, thus apparently condemning them to a life of innocence by robbing them of the power to choose, to act. The court rose, satisfied that the Law of Survival reigned supreme still in their ghostly brothers as in themselves. The cook and the steward, the sole possessors of the prize they all sought, as did their innocent observers, my substantial shadow among them. If he was innocent, I thought, then perhaps it was I myself in my doubts of him and his court who had incurred some stain of guilt in what I now saw to be my apparent condemnation of shadow and court. I awaited the sentence which took place the following day with some apprehension, much as Fielding had felt when his plan, once formulated, would first be brought to light when he enlisted part of the crew, his shadows, to help him.

******

The following morning the court assembled as before and we were there to hear the Chief Justice sentence the four deemed guilty. The master of hounds, the presiding presence in this legal Eden, began by citing the prisoners' change of plea regarding their part in Fielding's murder from not guilty to guilty They had thus acknowledged their crime and had been, he said, in so doing well advised. They were men, now, not shadows who hid in safety from the light–the morning sun shone brilliantly through the cathedral-like window into the Chief Justice's Eden. The four were adorned with the golden light, their long shadows stretched before them enveloping the prosecutor and the defence and reaching the foot of the jury box, the jury itself blinded by the light. The four heads before the court looked disturbingly golden and apple-like–they became acknowledged observers of their own actions, thus making what seemed one two, just as they had made two one by the axes they had wielded in the name of security. They seemed the Chief Justice's creatures, but he made them his creator, innocently enough, since only their guilt could validate the Law of safety which he defended through them. Without crime, needless to say, there would be no court; the court's existence depended entirely on the existence of the crime the court and the prisoners finally conspired together to make real by breaking the Revenue Laws of existence in their attempt to overthrow their own lives. He sought the treasure of safety in their guilt as they sought the *Saladin's* treasure in their mutiny; but all shared the desire for survival as they all shared the guilt.

In the Chief Justice's words, as he continued, there could have been no fear of apprehension, mentioned in their defence, for the attempt could not have been successful if it had not been carried out with consummate art. His words describe the condemnation in the trial of the men as it describes their actions on the *Saladin*–consummate art indeed which hides guilt under the robes of security! Safety was the fruit he sought, the treasure he created, the golden apple that had eluded the prosecutor and so saved him as he saved the cook and steward. But now the tree cultivated by the prosecutor was recreated in the Chief Justice's sentence. Addressing the four he continued and described their condition after the first night's murders–he was clearing and digging the earth around his tree, cultivating it and giving it the fertiliser which made it flourish. The tempting prize for which they had waded through all that blood was in their possession, but no sooner so than distrust and guilty fear had crept in among them, and had induced them to hurry the great seducer by whom they had been corrupted after the victims that had been cast into the sea. Fertiliser indeed–possession, suspicion and further mur- der–how closely this parallels the confession, trial and con- demnation the four men had undergone in the jail and court. They were, he said, upon the trackless deep, with all the world before them–the closing line of *Paradise Lost*. The four like the two exiled from the Garden of Eden, the Garden of the Law, the Chief Justice's Eden–which he was creating in his own image in the sentence he articulated.

Like the four in apparent possession of the *Saladin* and her treasure, the Chief Justice was well nigh in possession of the golden apple he and his court had struggled so long to bring to fruition. But, like him who addressed them further, they received no benefit from their treasure but were here to receive the sentence of death for coveting that to which they had no rightful claim! The golden apple is almost within his reach; he grasps it in his mind's hand. His hand touches it now as he passes the sentence of death by hanging on the four men: "these unhappy victims are hurried without warn- ing into the presence of their Maker." Their Maker was speak- ing to them, the creator of the legal Garden into which they were to be admitted under the kind auspices of its chief gar- dener. He had his four golden apples in his hands–all he need now do was to make them grow–their Maker, their Creator, their refuge, their safety. His last words were not without irony: "You will still have the aid of pious Clergymen to prepare your spirits for their final departure; in their hands I leave you." –it's almost like leaving Fielding in MacKenzie's hands as the *Saladin* prepared to sail, isn't it? Clergymen, those will- ing labourers in the Chief Justice's garden, those cultivators of the soiled soul which they laboured so diligently to make grow and flower, those apple-pickers extraordinary. Well, I've seen the seed, the planting, the cultivation, and the fruit. What remains is like seeing a dream of possession become possession itself, the exile's return to the Garden from which he was justly driven, a dream of creation become creation itself. And this is what followed on Tuesday, July 30.

After breakfasting, I followed my substantial shadow past the college on the north end of the Grand Parade. And then I continued past St. Paul's Church on the south to Sackville Street where his shadow fell before me struggling up the steep hill–college and church behind facing each other across the cultivated green grass of the Parade. It was a mutely eloquent sight shadowing forth the courtroom where the Chief Justice faced the four with his cultivated garden between them. We arrived at the junction of Albermarle and Sackville and were forced to stop. Two closed wagons proceeded slowly forward, turning left up Sackville toward the open fields beyond the street we trod. They had come from the jail and were proceeded by the High Sheriff, Mr. Sawyer, in a wig and were guarded by two ranks of soldiers, First Royals, appropriately named. They were the armed representatives of Queen and court, the armed protectors of a security they seemed to hold in doubt, if fixed bayonets were suitable upholders of peace and the Law. The sun shone bravely on the just and the unjust as my shadow fell in behind the column; and I, of course, followed suit as we traced the condemned men up the hill and into the cultivated fields toward an as yet unseen destination. We were following the last vestige of the *Saladin*, wrecked on the Harbour Island of safety, and slowly being ground to pieces by the rocky teeth of the Law. My shadow and I had boarded her, inventoried her cargo, listened to her Captain Johnston tell his tale which his men corroborated; and now we had returned to her remains from the court to see her a last time and also see, perhaps, her treasures at last.

The fields we passed through slowly behind the prisoners were marked here and there by magnificent trees from which cultivators had mercifully restrained their axes. The scene in the morning sun was idyllic, even pastoral, in its simplicity, a man-made Eden which showed, as the Garden of Adam and Eve apparently did not, a ready access and fruitful balance between axe, mattock and plow. On the one hand, tree, soil, and earth; on the other, man's hand on the tools he wielded to strike, cut and dig the earth into a fruitfulness he desired and got. Ahead now I saw a grove of young trees in greater number than I had seen around me before, and between us and the grove a cemetery. The shadows cast by the gravestones overshadowing the buried inmates, saving their eyes from the bright sun, shadows enshadowed, bearing the same relationship as I and my leading shadow did; only differing from them in our slow forward movement, prisoners of prisoners, seeking treasure. The grove drew closer now and I suddenly saw within its semicircle of trees the tree of knowledge, the tree I had envisioned in the court as I watched the Chief Justice and his gardeners cultivate it and bring it to fruition. Before me stood the fruits of their labours, the tree with four vertically hanging tendrils and from the end of each a tear-drop shaped now empty loop, the void circlet that is the only edible product this tree of safety provides. Beside the young trees in the grove around it, this tree looked grotesque, severely geometrical, a mad-man's dream of what a tree might look like after he, in his madness, had forgotten the trees he had once seen but no longer could. The tree which only circumstance could have created, the creator a man possessed, a man who found his life in circumstance, the golden apple of safety which made him as he had made it in his own shadowy image.

The prison wagons continued, as the First Royals did beside them. The High Sheriff left his gig and mounted the gallows-tree where the executioner, dressed in black to make even more emphatic his shadowy condition, awaited him. Two men of the cloth stood beside him, shadows too, whose labours in the Garden had set them here with the executioner, all three like black birds of prey perched in the branches of a tree they designed and built, awaiting quietly the fruits of that eternal task. Men of God, whether bench or pulpit, preaching the gospel of safety as if it were a private possession dispensed only on the Sabbath or in the Supreme Court. The three awaited Sawyer, who spoke briefly to them while the four descended to the earth from the wagons and passed slowly through the double file of First Royals. They left the earth behind them as they mounted the steps to the platform and were received by the four standing there to serve their turn upon them. Two ministers, an executioner and a High Sheriff shadowing forth Johnston and Hazleton, Jones and Anderson– the shadows seeking substance. Their chosen forms of security were before them as were the condemned men who submitted to their worship of safety by confessing and so living by the Law that the four shadows they faced only died by, men whose lack of choice was chosen by them. And then, the choosing forgotten, they lived only by the fruits of forgetfulness and the denial of choice to others.

The four who had come from the jail moved in accordance with the executioner's orders to stand beneath those vertical tendrils with their empty fruit hanging above the men's heads. They were dressed in prison gray, their faces wan and pale; the long ten-day wait since the sentence had been passed, apparently, in sleepless hunger, refusing the food they were offered as their spirits refused the sleep their bodies demanded–rebellious to the end. What had once been a common swarthiness, a deep tan, had, during the long wait, seemed to fade, to lose its evidence of sun and health and turn a golden green in the whispering semi-shade of the grove and the brightly shining morning sun. So much for their outward appearance. The expression on all their faces as they faced the crowds who came to witness their transformation was placid, and calm with the calmness of an object, an object which speaks in silence in the tones of its colour and the statement of its shape. All were calm, but only one was rigid, gazing out over the heads of the crowd, over the fields, the distant city, the ocean to the east, rigid and expressing in deafening silence indifference, indifference to men, to scene, to gallows, to death. It was Anderson, who, fiery avenger of the *Saladin* that he was, had acted to destroy the authority which he felt had wished to destroy him and so became the victim of the force he set out to kill. For him alone, it was not a transformation but simply a mockery of the condition in which he already existed. He had already placed the rope around his neck with his own hand. The others looked down into the crowd who must have looked shadowy to them, ghosts before the eyes of the living.

As they exchanged words with the two ministers standing before them, the executioner behind them placed the empty tears around their necks and all at once I saw the tree of knowledge, of the Law of safety, before me burst from angular and rigid sterility into fruitfulness. The men's heads were the green-golden apples the Chief Justice had brought to fruition on his tree in court. And here, instead of growing and emerging from the tree as they do in nature to provide food and nourishment to men, here, I say, I saw the fruit placed on the tree and attached there. The tree was the fruit of these heads in the logic of legal organic growth rooted in heaven and reaching toward the earth, tree from fruit, not fruit from tree. The Chief Justice and his gardeners sought the golden apple of safety by turning men into those golden apples upon which they intended to feed–unpalatable fare, to my mind–and in the court tried to establish their performance in the eyes of all as a naturally achieved fruition. Before my eyes I now saw the fruit bring forth the tree and my shadow disappeared although the sun shone still on the golden apples of the tree before me, unpicked. The fruit whose seed is in itself, whose growth is seen but whose source of growth is not, the shadow seen, the substance invisible. The shadow is the substance if the substance must be seen as invisible, like the yellowing leaves of a birch tree standing behind them, leaves and heads.

Before the executioner adjusted the ropes through the rings of the scaffold and prepared them for the drop, the four shook hands and bade each other farewell. Their hands joined, their shadows joined also giving voice to the last vestige of the separateness that is life, apparently, separateness seen in the unity of their past desires and actions and their present condition, so soon to be changed, I thought, or was it? How changed, if so? The four made last minute confessions, an echo of the former confessions that were followed by that other trial and now this present one. Johnston's words spoke for all: "I offer my life as a sacrifice for my misdeeds"–he still speaks of life as a possession to be given away, this time as a sacrifice–his possessiveness is the misdeed. His devotion to security finds him on the tree he brought to fruition, he, the creator, the fruit of his own creation–yet not creator, nor creature, but the eyes, his eyes, that he sees by means of and through at the same time. I am those eyes, watching him now as I watched him then–in him I saw *Saladin* and court as I see them now, in these, my written words. Now kneeling in prayer, heads covered by the yellow caps that shone dully in the sun, apples now without features, the ministers of the cloth hearing their last words–last words indeed! I'm here to belie that sentiment–the bar that supported the drop was removed and the golden apples attached to the vertical tendrils dropped heavily and swung, gently writhing, apples at last.The fruit of a tree which supported them from above but provided now no earthly platform, as in the *Saladin* they had sought support from above in dreams of security, wealth, guilt and protection under the Law. They found it, food for the Chief Justice's table to be shared by him with his ghostly associates whose work was completed in the natural grove beyond the city's walls.

The treasure of the *Saladin* I have survived to tell, counting, accounting for, in the dangerous safety of explanation the substance for which this inn can only be a shadow, its name, golden, the shining, the shadowy light which allows us to see while it prevents our knowing. A golden apple like those hanging in the grove, but not, like them, transformed into the life they sought ever elsewhere, ever exiled, ever seeking. Apparently they found what I see; my seeking is their finding–they show me the way, and I, in my way show it here. Some look to divinity to heaven, and I look to the earth, the shadow of that divinity whose light to me is shadow, the shadow of the *Saladin* and her crew, the men who are, at last, the treasure she carries still. The treasure, the object of the trial, I have tried to realise in this journal through an account of the legal scene in the court and its result. But the official trial, as I see it, is only a beginning with an end; my trial began before this last and I must render an account of it, too, if this would-be substance is to make visible the shadow and, finally, the light that creates them both. If the trial and execution I witnessed gives existence to the theory, the idea, then my actions that led to seeing the theory's existence in other words than sentencing will, perhaps, give some degree of shadowy substance to my own trial and its aftermath, my words.

haps it will bring the dilemma to light that has lain in my hold for so long, undelivered, and, in my case, unsuspected. Newspapers, those organs of information and reportage so dear to our–how shall I say–yes, our hearts began to arouse my interest. Late last May *The Nova Scotian* carried a somewhat vague account of a report given the editors by one Captain Cunningham, commanding the coastal schooner *Artemis* just arrived from Drumhead, a small port on Country Harbour. It

CHAPTER TWO

The Sentence

It is by the blessing of God that I come here. I have told some lies in order to conceal the things which have occurred, but I now wish to tell the truth in order to relieve my mind.

A Cook's Confession

The Golden Inn, Lunenburg, 7 August, 1844: The question I was left with yesterday haunts me still, if it can be called a question at all. Perhaps the moral dilemma of a trial and its unresolved ambiguity is more a burden that must be borne than an abstract problem requiring rational analysis, whether by legal authority or only by an observer like myself. The coin of righteousness weighs heavily, ballast for my sometimes top-heavy vessel's subjection to the fearful winds and rebellious seas I still navigate so precariously. My initial certitude was overcome by my desperate need to see myself, certain or not, in command of my world as I know it; but this desperation, in its turn, was overthrown because I cannot escape seeing desperation as a deficit in my accounting of the reasonable life I lead. Subjection to the need I felt was, I came to see, actually servitude which would rob me of my life if I didn't resist it–and so I did; I dropped the mask of desperation which concealed me from myself. What lay behind it was the man who had loved my former certitude as he had also felt my subsequent desperation. But now he had emerged;

he had command of his world as he knew it, and I was the observer of this shadow, unseen and critical, thus divided from him. I was, myself, apparently incapable of further action, relegated to detachment and passivity, while, at the same time, being carried forward toward an unknown destination. An unhappy state, I must confess; seemingly fixed and static like an island in the sea, a threat to safe navigation, when, as it is in my case, unknown, uncharted.

The *Saladin's* case, as I have shown, was strangely mine. The stranger I met through her case was, of course, the man I observed and still observe as myself; the observer, then, and the man, myself, gave rise to a third: the eye that sees the other two, my self and observer. How did this triangle arise, I may ask again, even after I have told so much? Perhaps my vision is impaired; perhaps it only appears to be as clear as it does. I need to make it clearer as I once needed to see when I was only man and observer, Ahab, under Elijah's reproof. The possession of Naboth's vineyard, one recalls, was the issue: Jezebel showed Ahab the way to what he wanted, and Ahab took it. Well, the need for resolution of the paradox found in my feeling at one with the *Saladin's* complement, living and dead, is Naboth's vineyard. Ahab, Jezebel and Elijah figure forth for me my being, divided as I have described, into three uneasy parts. But what on earth has Ahab to do with Soloman Scharf, a man from Lunenburg, who teaches and sometimes talks, sometimes writes? And furthermore, if Ahab's tale is unrelated to Scharf, then what, in God's name, is this damning sense of oneness the beggar feels with the obvious remoteness of a case of mutiny, piracy and murder! Perceiving my reluctant recognition of the paradox, and asking for renewed courage, I now intend to retrace the genesis of my meeting, my exchange and my sentence. The telling is my last hope; in it, I trust, my sentence lies.

If I can make clear my reasons for walking to Halifax last month to attend the trial of the *Saladin's* survivors, per-

seemed a barque, the *Saladin*, had run ashore under full sail on the southern tip of Harbour Island. The ship was manned by six men; their officers and additional crew had, they claimed, deserted the *Saladin* at sea; she carried a cargo of guano, copper, silver ingots and $10,000 in cash. I quickly condemned the six as pirates and probably mutineers. A day later more details appeared not only in *The Nova Scotian* but also *The Morning Post*; my curiosity was further inflamed, and my condemnation of the survivors found fresh impetus. A week later, *The Halifax Herald* told of the arrival of the *Fair Rosamund* at Halifax from Country Harbour carrying the prisoners and the money from the wrecked barque. I began to feel a sense of doubt which led me to question my previous judgment of the six men. Prisoners and money made a thought-provoking cargo; had my judgment, passed, as it had been, so summarily, been in the interests of justice in our society, or for my own profit in the coin of righteousness? Surely it was justice; the case was clear enough. But then, were newspaper reports reliable evidence? Or was evidence actually newspaper reports, the reporting of an event by an observer whose eyes were only someone else's, in this case Cunningham's? A doubt persisted in my mind; I was arraigned in my own court of Law, my God-given intelligence questioned my reason for an alleged crime: the vanity of the human wish to be right above all things. Thus my judgment and my intelligence met face to face. The former was in control; intelligence was accused of ignoring Law, or calling authority into question. Thus my formerly unquestioned powers of judgment met a stranger in my midst whose not inconsiderable authority, in spite of its alleged crime, had to be recognised. The arraignment ended, the trial was to take place at an indefinite future time and place.

And then, two weeks later, *The Morning Post* printed Carr's and Galloway's confessions; apparently, this confirmed my powers of judgment. Here was conclusive evidence of guilt beyond a doubt. The cook and the steward made my judgment unquestionable by acquiescing in its rectitude. But didn't this shadow forth what I myself, the stranger, had done in believing in my own condemnation of the survivors earlier on journalistic evidence? This thought threw me once again into arraignment. Must I confess myself a distinct, however distant, cousin if not brother of a mutinous cook and a steward? Nearly a month passed; and during that time, I wrestled with my suspicion, my burden. At last I decided, and the forces of Law carried me under guard to Halifax to appear before the bar as an observer tried severely by my questioning judgment. Guilt was not the least valuable item in my Bill of Lading.

I began the walk to Halifax on the tenth of the month. Even at six in the morning, the sun was making itself felt as I headed roughly north and east toward Mahone Bay and Chester where I planned to spend the night at Isaac's farm. Isaac's son was a former student of mine. My route followed the shoreline for the most part; the sea breeze kept the heat of the day under control. The path wasn't any more arduous than usual, blocked as it often is by stumps in varying degrees of decay with the stump-tops painted red, looking disconcertingly like the necks of decapitated outlaws. But in spite of such obstacles, I made good progress. The sea, on my right hand, glittered in the sun and recalled to mind the *Saladin's* case that set me on my present course of action. The weeds, on my left, were thick, sunlight only reaching down through summer leaves to the ground and trunks in truant beams and an irregular mark and bright network of shifting shapes. I walked between sea and forest with a sense of confident anticipation. The confessions I had read in *The Morning Post* nourished my faith in my powers of judgment; the exercise and the fresh air stimulated me, and I began silently reproving myself for questioning or even feeling doubt about so clear a case, or so guilty a crew. Their punishment would be swift and severe, I said to myself. The instinct that put my reason to the test was no more than a passenger without the authority to interfere in the strength and virtuous exercise of judgment. Each alternate foot-fall on the path brought me on my way: thus balanced and active, I stood and walked on my two legs which carried forward the form and force of reason. Nourished by such thinking, I crossed the Mushamush, stopping only for a draught of cool well-water at a farmhouse on a hill giving a view of Mahone Bay to the east. The well was behind the house; no one was in evidence. A dipper hung on the well frame from which a bucket was suspended like a hanged culprit on the rope that had throttled him for justice's sake. I looked around but no one appeared, so I drew some water and drank. I hadn't remembered how thirsty walking made me. Refreshed, I continued on in the heat, having removed my coat and stowed it in the back-satchel that contained a change of linen, my razors, and a modest supply of food.

Drawing closer to Mahone Bay by noon, I began to feel hungry. The heat had intensified and my legs told me to rest for a time. I obeyed the commands of stomach and legs, whose ultimate authority we men only question at our peril, found a shady recess off the path, and sat down to take my noon meal. My body served my purpose, and now I, in turn, served it by responding to its requirements, a cook and steward at the same time. My purpose, the establishment of the security of righteousness, enforced recognition of the flesh and blood that must be fostered if the purpose was to be achieved. But what was this purpose, finally, but the survival of what could only be justly described as an idea? Instinct spoke in me again, though faintly–an instinctive birth of vague fear before the glory of an ideal, such as *Diana* must have seemed to *Actaeon*, an ideal of justice, which fed upon the flesh and blood it condemned, finding vitality in what it opposed. A sapling, green and flourishing, stood by the side of a red-painted stump in the path near where I sat; the seed, turned in the earth, had forced itself through that earth and had risen above that which opposed its growth, yet it drew its strength from that same earth. If the tree were to live, the earth must live too, if only to feed the tree. My feelings about reason and judgment, tested by the *Saladin*'s case, had impelled me to take the journey to the capital, in many ways a return to the security of home for me, as it has subsequently proved. But wasn't I seeing justice like a sapling whose roots were in the sky–a tree without an earth to nourish its growth; or reason without instinctive intelligence to give it life? Perhaps, but now I once again began to question; the voice that spoke to my reason was the passenger still, but a passenger with some authority. I found myself listening to that ironic questioning of reason like one might listen to a ghostly voice echoing through a weatherproof but empty house.

As I rose to journey on, I heard and looked up to see a red-headed woodpecker vigorously and repeatedly driving his beak into the bark of an ancient maple, from the hole in which he would eventually draw an insect, his food. Far from the earth, the bird had found nourishment. Not without reason I found food for thought in this, food that strengthened me to continue my journey toward what seemed to me then to be a well-established destination. I was unaware of the axe I wielded that severed tree from earth, and then shaped that tree and others to suit the woodsman's, the carpenter's, or the shipbuilder's purposes. The ship has yet to be built that will carry us in safety to the refuge our purposes create for us to rest in. And it was rest I sought, the long day's walk having sapped my strength as the sun neared the western horizon. I followed my lengthening shadow into the shelters which men built near to one another and named Chester. It was dark now among the trees, though their tops were golden yet, and dark along the shadowy path that led me to Isaac's farm, where I was welcomed warmly by father and son, while the mother busied herself in preparing an added place at their generous supper table. We ate and talked as the light waned outside and the lamps were lit to circle our way to bed. A cot near the fireplace was prepared for me. The fire burned low, banked for the night, ready to be relit for the morning's repast–my sapling's fate in the scheme of things; my searching during the day's walk had showed me the illicit nature of attempting to satisfy my instinctive questioning at the expense of governing reason. It had, at the same time, brought about the meeting of these two captains of the soul. I slept.

The sleep of the just is dreamless, and I woke early renewed in limb and spirit. The Isaac family rose at sun-up, and we ate a hearty porridge. The father and son soon departed to continue clearing their land, an endless task boding no good to tree, bush and shrub that encroached on the farmer's lot. I thanked them all for their generous welcome and hospitality. They had heard of the *Saladin* through newspaper reports and shared my view of it as an example of God's Law and the unity of human attempts to violate it for one's own profit. But they didn't share my doubt, and so I kept it to myself. The simplicity of their life, like the simplicity of their reasoning, shone forth in the energy they displayed in labouring to make their farm the Lord's vineyard; Isaac was a Naboth free of a covetous Ahab or an unscrupulous Jezebel. I wished them well and started toward Hubbard's, twelve miles to the east along the shore. The road (or more properly the bridle path) stretched ahead, marked, as my yesterday's path had been, by stubborn rocks and the ever-present red-painted stumps. Turning into the path, I looked back over my left shoulder to wave farewell to Isaac; he returned the gesture, but his son's axe could be heard already, attacking the first of the many trees he would sentence and execute that day.

Yesterday's sun was hidden behind today's heavy overcast, making its heat felt nonetheless. A south-west wind strong enough to turn the lighter tree tops to whips drove the low hanging clouds fitfully before it. The day gave promise of rainfall that wasn't long in coming. My coat was stout and a wide-brimmed hat would protect my head from all but the most violent downpour. And fortunately, when it did start to rain an hour after my departure from Isaac's farm, it was a light, though steady, fall. It was one of those grateful summer rains that slake the thirst of trees and growing things. The wood's population, represented to my sight yesterday by a lone red-headed woodpecker, appeared in the form of porcupine, squirrel and deer brought out by the rain, I supposed, to share its rejuvenating powers with other forms of organic life that gave them food unstintingly. I must have seemed an interloper to them. They stopped and watched my strange figure, all but engulfed by the clothing I wore to protect me from the very elements that brought them life; a ghost wandering in exile through a land that I and my kind must have seemed bent upon enslaving for our own purposes. The path I followed appeared to me like the scarred wound it was, inflicted by the minds and axes of men who cut the bridle paths to permit them passage. I represented them all, making a home in the natural world which was a refuge against that world by the single, dividing stroke of a weapon whose materials had come from the very source they were turned upon to create further shelter, further protection in the name of security. The path and my presence along it, the red-painted stumps glistening in the rain, beheaded trees, seemed a violation, a physically brutal assault on life itself in destruction only seen to be ironic in the light of its purpose, creation or, more properly, security. I stopped momentarily under the leafy tent of a maple; a doe moved cautiously but without fear out of the dark interior of the forest to look at the interloper whose two legs and hairless exterior proved him to be an alien from an unknown land. I stood stock-still; perhaps he was an unfamiliar kind of tree, she thought. Minutes passed; the doe drew near, no more than two feet from me. I extended an open hand to touch her–an unexpected movement from a tree–and she darted away deep into the forest. She sensed an inimical

ing, and her instinct seemed to have saved her life; I watched her shadowy form until it disappeared among the musty trees and stepped once more into the path, as ghostly as the animal I had quite naturally conjured into invisibility.

The feeling of alienation, even exile, that this encounter gave rise to continued as I strode on; carefully avoiding stump and stone, the earth's revenge on the unwary traveller whose unwelcome presence is suffered patiently but not always passively by the land he invades. This alienation was the alienation of a condemned man, outside the Law which has passed judgment on him and sentenced him to imprisonment; the prison walls were formed by the blows of axe and maul as he created out of the natural world a shelter from it. His attempt to escape it only served to enclose him the more rigidly. But the ravages he perpetrated were in their turn overcome by the continuity to be seen in nature, that same continuity also found in the generations of men. Escape came, therefore, once again through the very nature that man violated to form his shelter that had, in turn, imprisoned him, apparently. This double continuity provides the limits that confine the confinement man seems to live within and so provides, ironically enough, the escape he seeks so fervently with axe and maul. Natural life, then, reveals the Law in its every tree, bird and animal. The Law of man, on the other hand, seemed to manifest itself only in the action of creative axe dividing and so preserving. A form of self-preservation based upon bodily assault and heedless violence, a degrading manifestation of authority which belied its dignity and force by the form which its exercise took. My encounter with the doe led me thus to ruminate as I continued along the path, crossing the East River by means of a rude bridge of logs bound precariously together by the twisted bark of trees. The bridge safely traversed, I approached Hubbard's through continuing mist and rain, feeling in my self a spanning of the gap between what the doe revealed and he who received that tion. My pining search for rectitude had permitted my self to seem a bridge over the gulf that divided the doe and the exile.

The hour of noon brought me to Hubbard's; and a sudden opening in the forest revealed the gray, wind-stirred sea under rain clouds whose hues matched exactly those of the sea below them. This uniformity of colour was shaded to the darkness of the forest through intervening patches of fog and mist. Looking ahead along the path, my eyes were greeted by a startling sight. An extensive stand of red maples, running from the beach into the deep forest and extending as far as the eye could see along the path, contrasted strongly with the grayness of sea and sky and blackness of the trees. It flamed out in variegated shades of red, an inferno of colour, burning without heat amid rain and mist, a seeming land of fire. I passed into it, the path dictating my route forward, until, on my left I saw, formed by a huge fallen tree, a cave-like shelter. The roots of the tree rose twelve feet into the air; the hollow left would protect me from the weather while the food I carried would preserve me from the hunger and growing fatigue my forenoon walk had caused. Natural shelter outside me, and man-made food (a sort of shelter) inside me showed me the bridge I was. As axe bites tree to form path and house, so my teeth bit into black bread and cheese to preserve my life and strength. Satisfied, I decided to rest for a time before resuming my journey. Comfortably protected from the persistent rain and wind, my thoughts turned again to the doe's revelations to the ghostly exile. I seemed to be traversing a forest, but the path was no more; as I moved rapidly through the underbrush, I found I was making my own path simply by following a direction which static tree and thorny bush could not effectively block. Mist made the forest warm and dank.

Suddenly, at some distance before me I saw, standing under a sheltering maple, a dark threatening shape, tall, but without branches or leaves, unmoving–two devouring eyes pierced me. How could it remind me of a tree, of whatever berevelasort, if it had eyes? Still, its fixity allayed the fears the eyes had stimulated. I stepped nearer; part of it moved, extending something pale toward me, almost touching me. I turned and ran without looking back, but the eyes pursued me still. I saw them staring at me as I sunk deeper and deeper into the forest, my shelter and fostering mother. As I ran, the eyes faded gradually; but I heard a voice coming from the mist around me. "Trees live as you live, by God's creative act and the Law, which is embodied in the flesh by and in which you live, the Law itself. Fear not!" My eyes opened slowly to look into the single eye of the mist-shrouded sun, which struggled to pierce the shroud by dissipating the opaque layer of vapour that divided it from the earth it gratefully nourished with heat and light. I had slept and the devouring eyes still resonating before me gradually became the single eye that had now early dispersed the mist, its brightness forcing me to squint to avoid its unaccustomed glare. I arose from my shelter comforted to see the sun again and feel its heat. The natural shelter of my cave-like hollow was now to be found in the open, undiscriminating light. The voices of invisible birds, the rustling of unseen animals accompanied me as I journeyed on. A pervading sense of harmony with the natural scene enhanced the energy I had gained from food and rest. My former sense of exile and alienation, of being an outlaw had apparently vanished; a red-painted stump I stepped aside to avoid showed three valiant sprouts of bright green growing; the axe was defeated! Its spectral wielder seemed suddenly weak in his savagery, passive in his self-preserving assaults, ghostly in his physical strength. I followed his path not because I was under its dominion but because it served my purpose. The path was mine. It led me to the Supreme Court and Commons of my capital.

The heat of the early afternoon sun soon dried my coat and hat, and told me to remove and stow the coat away. I walked through fog-like mist that rose from earth, stump, tree and underbrush still wet from the recent rain. The sense of harmony between me and my surroundings continued to grow. Geldert's busy inn surrounds me now; but then it seemed as remote, as unfamiliar, even as spectral as that wood's path near Ingraham's River seems to me now. What I saw in the capital, ahead of me then, has perhaps made this hostelry into a supreme court. The ale I drank at supper recreates the harmony I felt as I crossed Ingraham's River to a new sound from a new world, at any rate seemingly new to me then in my doe-like harmoniousness. It was the discordant sound of voice and axe, the one felling my harmony while the other downed the trees. I gazed ahead through the luminous rising mist. Perhaps two hundred yards ahead, ghostly shapes moved as one might imagine the damned to move about their hopeless because endless labours in a strange Hades where Sisyphus's tasks were performed in the midst of Elysian Fields, his weary feet crushing the fragrant asphodel as he laboured. Inarticulate voices, hardly human to my ear, reached me; drawing closer, the sunlight caught and flashed on something above the low-lying mist moving in an arc which began silently in the mist and ended there too with a sharp tearing thump. I stopped. Who were these invaders? What did their voices tell? The impulse to turn and run for my life was equalled by natural curiosity. It wasn't fear, but reluctant shyness, an unwillingness to forego harmony to gain knowledge that slowed my steps. While I continued, nonetheless, toward the sounds until they were incarnated before my eyes, the mist became men like myself, the sounds became the flesh of living men who worked with tools to widen and then clear my path.

There were four of them, two wielding axes, the others struggling to move to the roadside felled trees and stumps ripped from the fostering earth. A few hundred feet further along what could now be safely styled a road were two more men working with spades filling the holes left by the stumps. The four I approached first, appearing out of the mist, stopped and stared, wide-eyed, at the phantom that stood before them, apparently conjured forth from the earth or the forest, weightless and travel-stained. Then one laughed, soon to be joined by his fellows; the phantom was soon cut down to size and the degree of their fear was measured by the heartiness of their laughter when knowledge replaced wonder. I exchanged greetings with them; their voices sounded harsh and foreign to me; but I soon became accustomed to them, as they did to me. They had come west from Halifax and were, they said, employed by the colonial government to improve–strange choice of words, I thought–to improve the road. Soon, they boasted, Geldert's stage line would be running coaches from the capital to Hubbard's, even to Chester and beyond. Ships of the road drawn by animals yoked and harnessed in the interest of getting from one place to another–but from where, and to what destination, none had paused to consider. In their words I saw my harmony transmogrified; oneness with nature here became bondage to man's purpose, strength reduced by subjection to abject servitude. Freedom became bondage– the vision of a stage and its horses figured forth harmony, but harmony of coercion, of tyranny in which rode, in limited comfort, the blind lord of the world he served. And these men were preparing his way, making straight in the desert the highway for his lord. Desert indeed! And men in name only, being, as they seemed to me, exiled invaders of a land they chose not to see as anything more than an obstacle to their and others' purposes. I saw the tree he felled and he who felled it as one. They apparently saw me as one of them. I never felt more alien and vulnerable than I did when their friendliness became clear to me. But I made use of it for my own purposes, nevertheless, asking if there might be accommodation along the road ahead.

They directed me to Jacob's, a farm which the enterprising owner, hearing of the plans for a stage road at his front door, had quickly ceased farming and turned his house into a hostelry for travellers. The place, they said, was some nine miles ahead, on the eastern bank of the Indian River. My repeater told me it was four o'clock; with my path become a road, I could reach Jacob's before nightfall for a meal and much needed rest. I thanked them for their information and said farewell to men with whom I had never felt the touch of harmony and so had never met–the farewell was a mere form without substance, empty, a pretence. With the sun behind me, I followed my slowly lengthening shadow along the now uneven but at least unobstructed roadway. Former harmony seemed less in evidence, slowly becoming more a dread-like memory though still present as I walked onward. "Where yuh bound?" "To Jacob's!" It was the two with spades pausing in their work of filling holes and looking, for all the world, like energetic sextons filling in the graves of substanceless corpses, ironically their own. I passed on without further exchange, and left them behind me, creators of what for them and their masters was a flowering desert; but what for me was an impossible wilderness robbed of its natural harmony, an image without a soul. They were blind pirates whose crimes were seen as improvements, whose savagery was reason, and whose violence was Law under which they enslaved themselves and called it freedom, even progress. I was free, but not with their freedom, condemned by them to exile, perhaps; but still free with my sense of harmony and life that divided us, it seemed, forever. The bridge between doe and exile I had seen was replaced by the gulf I now perceived between me and the men I turned my back upon.

The late afternoon sun was sinking low, the shadows lengthened and I followed mine where that shadow led me, pointing the way to Indian River, not far ahead now. I could sense, if not see, the gap in the forest the river made, a valley between nearer and more distant tree-tops a few hundred yards away. A short interval brought me to the riverbank; the log bridge, dilapidated and showing gaping holes, was clearly impassable. A small skiff on the far bank, though not distant, must be a ferry of sorts. But where was the boatman, the Charon of that Indian Styx? I looked around for some sign or clue to help me resolve my dilemma. Above me to the left I saw a large, rusty iron triangle suspended from a tree-branch, with a rod of the same material hanging beside it. I raised raucous echoes in the forest by the vigour of my signalling, but no response seemed forthcoming. Lengthening shadows foretold sundown, and half-an-hour had passed before the clatter of oars in thole-pins answered my long-silenced signal. The vigorous oarsman soon crossed the river, beached his boat and turned to me. "A shilling in advance," was all he said. Exorbitant it was, but I was in no position to object; I paid and we soon reached the other side. My conductor was a middle-aged, strongly built man of swarthy complexion, black hair and beard, and dark piercing eyes. His name was Jacob, the farmer turned innkeeper I sought. He had turned from field to fireside, from profit found in growing, living things to what he clearly hoped would be a greater profit found in men who travelled. Men and potatoes led Jacob to the same desired end. I introduced myself to him and told him of my needs. Yes, he had room for me; his interest had increased as soon as I made myself known as a customer. I replied to his customary inquiries briefly. My day's journey and its events had been long and, I now felt, wearying. Jacob's obvious interest in money and in little else I found distasteful; like the men I saw on the road, he was slave to a master who was substanceless, and whose servant's life was reduced by his own will to a medium of exchange. I paid him in advance as we approached his hostelry. It was partially hidden by rising ground and a thick grove of trees that surrounded it off my road to the left in the gathering gloom.

The house was a one-storey structure built entirely of logs. Two small windows on either side of the entrance showed the faint reddish flicker that bespoke a fire inside. A circular hole cut in the door about the size of the ring-bolt on a hatch glowed with golden light and bore a disconcerting (though telling) resemblance to a golden sovereign. In the dusk the house, sunken in a hollow as it was and formed of moss-covered logs, looked as if it had grown from seed out of the earth in which it seemed to root itself. I was reminded of my noontide cave and my dream; it was here I was to find rest and sustenance to carry me on to the capital tomorrow. My host opened the door and I followed him into a clean, square, cell-like space. A pine table stood between the door and a stone fireplace in the opposite wall. The table bore an oil lamp; its light had turned the hole in the door to gold. On either side of the fireplace was a door that led to rooms beyond the one in which we stood. Beside the left-hand door I noticed the tools of a carpenter: two axes, a maul, and adze, plane and square. The room showed evidence of Jacob's skill; a half-finished table to the right awaiting its legs rested on the seats of four simply constructed chairs. More of these chairs were set against the central table and I took one gratefully. On further inspection, the room we occupied revealed little of note other than the expected furnishings of what had been the central room of a farmhouse now being converted into the public room of a roadside inn. What struck me most about it were not its furnishings, but the geometric symmetry that the space revealed, lighted as it was by the steady lamp flame and the flickering firelight. This symmetry found its final expression in a picture that hung over the square fireplace. A steel engraving of *Actaeon* peering through the trees and underbrush at an imperious *Diana*, both of whom were forever enclosed in a perfectly circular frame seemed to sum up the room, the house, and, perhaps, Jacob himself.

After a hearty supper of heavy stew and light ale, fatigue overcame me; and, at my request, my host showed me to my sleeping quarters, leading me through the door to the right of the fireplace. Lighting a taper on a bedside table, he bade me goodnight and left. The day's journey had been a long one; the bridge at Ingraham's River, that between the doe and the exile, had faded to became the gulf I had seen between the road workers and myself, the discord that changed former harmony into a memory. The gulf crossed by boat because of a impassable bridge had led me to food and now rest under the roof of a avaricious farmer turned innkeeper; the symmetry of the principal room and the interior of the house was masked by its strangely organic exterior. It was a shelter I had paid dearly for, necessary as it was; the taper sputtered and went out as my eyes closed in grateful sleep. A ghostly stag pursued by dog-headed men drifted and swirled before my uneasy eyes, slowly changing to a golden river in which was discovered, oars in thole-pins poised to row, an unmanned boat.

Jacob's movements in the main room awakened me. My sleep had hardly been dreamless, but it had restored my energies. I was soon sitting opposite my host eating, as I had at Isaac's the day before, a strength-giving porridge. The windows by the entrance were small and gave little illumination– the fire to my right still was the principal source of light for the occupants of the room. We ate in stony silence, and, soon finished, I rose and took my leave of a man I felt loath to see again, but my return journey, of course, would require it, whether or no. Yes, I was to pass this way again if Lunenburg was to be the home it is for me.

Walking once again in the early morning sun, my shadow behind me, my destination was seemingly within reach. I felt an exhilaration that reminded me of the sense of harmony I had felt the previous day. This was enhanced, too, by my turning my back on Jacob's and his travellers' farm. I looked back over my shoulder at the structure behind the trees in the hollow; it still looked as if it were growing out of the ground, but, beyond the grove of pines surrounding it, I saw some of what Jacob had tried to farm. The trees and thick had forest growth I had passed through the day before had here begun to thin out. Stunted pines and twisted alders struggled toward the sun through soil studded with rock, stone and boulder. The richness of vegetation farther west was showing increasing signs of poverty, even barrenness. Perhaps Jacob's change in means to profit had a deeper motive than the stony avarice I had seen in him the day before. What had to me seemed violence and destruction in the road workers, and once again in what Jacob had seemed the same to me last night, took on a changed significance now, seen again in the light of day. Jacob sought desperately for the coin of survival; he clung to anything and anyone from whom he could exact a toll. Whether from earth or traveller made no difference to him. His was, indeed, a stony, stubborn soil that no harrowing by implement or traveller could cultivate. On the rock of survival he had founded his life, and had, it seemed, rebelled against his nature and himself to transform whatever he found to gold, an alchemist caught in his own retort. And I had shared his food and his shelter, feeling still the gulf that divided me from him as it had from the road builders before. I was in exile yet.

The open road that led me to the head of St. Margaret's Bay was free of stumps; but they were succeeded by rocks that made walking almost as difficult as before. The poverty-stricken soil I had observed around Jacob's became more and more noticeable as I moved along. The terrain further west had been moderately level; but now, farther east, it became hilly. And as I clambered along the rocky slopes, I suddenly came upon what I might with justification call a mountain. My road rounded its base, eventually leaving the sea behind to turn south of east. I would see the sea again at the capital, but the height of the mountain on my left would give me a perspective for which I felt an inexplicable need. My route from the west had been largely masked by the trees of the forest which had given me the harmonious perspective that I had found in these natural surroundings. But it had perhaps been lost to a more restricted view seen in my judgment on the men I had met along the way. The western path had been widened by their labours, but I took a narrower view, ending, as it had, under Jacob's confining care. Stumps had become stones, and now I made them serve my turn as steps to take me to the mountain-top. They permitted me to pass, but with a tacit reluctance. It was an arduous climb and, inevitably, it recalled Hill Difficulty to me; but it seemed Christian's destination lay behind me and I was heading for what seemed his City of Destruction, having begun in the green forest. And now I was entering a stony barren stretch of land at the end of which lay the capital. The attempt to rise above the sense of confinement I felt from what I styled a stony narrowness of my view was taxing. My arms and legs were aching, the back-satchel was becoming an increasingly bothersome burden, my breathing was hard and my face was wet with sweat. But the stones made me see; I reached the summit, lay my burden down, sat on a convenient boulder and looked west toward invisible Lunenburg to see Mahone Bay, a gray-blue mist in the distance, divided from me and Margaret's by a green peninsula shining with morning light.

The expanse of the bay in the middle distance glittered golden and blue, a harder light which contrasted sharply with the softer shining green of the peninsula. At my feet far below was my winding road circling the foot of the mountain through sparse and sickly green scrub dominated by the whitish grey of the stony land. Turning east toward the sun and the distant capital, invisible but ever-present, I saw the terrain continue its stony way dotted here and there by what later proved to be the shelters of poverty-stricken farmers. My commanding view embraced the visible world and I felt its life; my isolation on the mountain top showed the perspective I had lived through, walked through and now had seen through– I was my perspective and the mountain upon which I stood put me in possession of that perspective. Thus fostered and sheltered by the natural stone supporting me, my sense of isolation, of exile was, it seemed, my freedom. I had crossed the line into a new world of which the old had been the creator, but that creator was now a ghost, vanishing in the light that he had articulated. The new world was mine to order, to command, to live in–the law was mine to exercise as I saw fit. And this new freedom appeared first in my suddenly feeling disembodied, weightless; the stone on which I leaned became shadowy–I no longer felt its roughness, its harshness. Who on earth was that spectre supported by a cloud? Where he had come from, I felt I knew; it was a gray-blue mist, and, passing through a green shining, he had evolved into a golden blue and whitish-gray to his present shadow, black against the gray-white, rock-shaped mist. I moved and he followed, descending from the heights slowly but surely, fearlessly, without questioning the solidity of the cloud upon which he found so precarious a footing.

Reaching the road again, his road, I proceeded forward with my shadow flowing, insinuating itself between and over rock and earth, following me as it grew shorter and shorter. On either hand now, the road revealed small, for the most part dilapidated, farm-houses. Gray occupants sometimes waved and my shadow returned their greetings. More than one farmer was employed working wood into fish-box or barrel; staves, hoops and heads lay about the feet of their maker, together with piles of shavings that were all that remained of the stock of wood that was their invisible source. These farms, generally, were in poor condition, shadowing forth in movement and activity the poverty of the stony shadows they attempted to cultivate. The scene reminded me of a new Hades populated by Rhadamanthine men whose transportation to the Elysian Fields had come about through their apparently profound desire to make their dying a living reality. They were to make ghostly stones and shadowy earth produce spectral food, just as they attempted to make trees into barrels, fish-boxes and shelters. Their walls became their life, inhabited by the ghostly prisoners of their own judgment and choice. And my shrinking shadow was one with them, differing only in his movement along the road in contrast with their apparent fixity.

My shadow and I climbed a long hill together and, reaching its summit, we saw before us an expanse of water, blue and glittering gold in the noon sun. It was the head of Black Point Lake, a short distance away to the east, ringed by green alders and scrub pine. Further to the south, separated from the lake before us by more misty stone, shone, blindingly, another larger lake. Beyond this, the shimmering light made whatever was there invisible, but I know I stood in what was becoming well-nigh unbearable heat before my destination, some twelve to fourteen miles away, whether invisible or not. The vision of water so near at hand raised thirsty thoughts, and I turned off the road south west to the edge of Black Point Lake. A convenient rock-shaped ledge sloping into the water gave me easy access to the cool lake water. I walked to the edge of the rock, knelt on it, catching my forward tending weight on my hands; my shadow was beneath me on the rock, the sun overhead. As I leaned forward, imaged by my shadow, I suddenly saw before my eyes that black shape take on the wavering features of a man with an elongated face, acquiline nose, dark hair and piercing black eyes staring at me from beneath the surface of the water. His mouth was open and lips extended as if preparing to drink. If he were to drink, it would be my substance that would slake his thirst, just as I would imbibe his shadow if I, in turn, should do the same. The shining surface of the pure water seemed to join shadow and substance, my image and I, as it clearly divided us. I was seeing my self before me, a shining vision; I drank–coolness and relief pervaded me.

As I closed my eyes, feeling as if I were somehow suffering transformation, my strangely embodied shadow seemed to disappear in the wavelets my drinking had caused. As I was an obstacle between sun and earth creating my shadow; so the water was an obstacle between me and my image, creating us in a dividing shimmer. Our living was the water; our seeing was the drinking of it. Thus refreshed, I rose and returned to the road turning right. The sun was now overhead; I had absorbed my shadow, or, at least I was standing over him. He had become, for the time, an invisible, solid support upon whom I stood. As I walked on, I looked again to the south east; the shimmering curtain of sunlight still seemed to conceal my destination–or did it? The light in the air above the earth recalled the shining surface of the lake where, so recently, I had felt I was somehow transformed, losing the freedom I came upon on the mountain. Behind the two shining surfaces there was in the first a face, and behind the other a city, the capital, my destination which would soon swallow me.

Rounding a bend in the road, I came upon another farmhouse much like those I came upon earlier. This one, on the left, however, showed a difference. Over the front entrance was a sign bearing crudely executed black letters on whitewash: Johnston's meals. The sentence called forth my appetite, or that of my invisible shadow who momentarily showed himself on the door under the sign before which I stood awaiting an answer to my knock. It opened quickly to occupy the space my shadow filled with a bold, red-haired, blue-eyed tanned farmer whose speech revealed his English origin; "Step in," he said, standing to one side.

I entered to find myself in a small, windowless room containing a large deal table and six wooden chairs, a wooden shelf on the wall opposite the entrance and, over it, an open sliding panel through which I could see someone moving about before a black rusted stove. The room had the smell of stale food and tobacco about it, giving a rather unpromising prospect of the forthcoming meal I expected. "We have oat cakes and tea, if that suits you–it'll have to." My host spoke with a voice more in command than inquiry; but my shadow answered silently advising me to eat this provender whether I liked it or not. I took a seat at the table, having nodded assent to the man called Johnston, and awaited my noon meal with some impatience; hunger seemed to confine me, an obstacle to my progress, and I still had a good twelve miles to go. Clattering from the kitchen foretold quick service. A plate of oat-cakes appeared through the service panel by a bodiless hand and forearm. Johnston placed it before me, and the molasses-sweetened tea which followed. The cakes were raw and the tea luke warm, the spectre of a decent meal, but I ate, thus gratefully acknowledging my shadow's commands and carrying them out loyally. I soon exorcized the contents of the plate and cup, paid my bill, and left Johnston's behind, considering that his boastful sign was a clear case of indigestible perjury; there seems to be no weightier spectre than a raw oat cake.

My road turned to the south of east now, and I found myself in a continuing rocky terrain that began a slow uneven downward slope toward Bedford Basin. I passed more lakes, smaller than those I had seen before, which appeared on either side of the road, as did the occasional farm. As time passed and the sun descended toward the western horizon, I was entranced by the reappearance of my shadow no longer following now, but leading me, however obliquely. Perhaps Johnston's cakes affected my eyes as they had my digestion; but I felt that shadow, even saw it, it seemed, beginning to show signs of substance. A feeling of coercion arose in the relationship between us; he led and I followed, indentured to a substanceless unforgiving master. The food I had eaten in his apparent absence had now given gradual rise to this new being I had first perceived against the shadowy rock on the mountain-top. Now my mountain freedom was becoming another state at a less elevated altitude; had I, or was I losing that life, that perspective? The sharp brightness and heat of early afternoon softened to a golden glowing as I approached MacGregor's Paper Mill a few hundred yards from the Basin. Trees to paper to print. Once again the fate of my erstwhile sapling recurred to me, growing evidence of life stretching heavenward from the earth from which it sprung, from black earth to the white upon the whiteness of paper. Thus from the mill that fed on the tree came the matter that gave to give its owner the food he sought, whether temporal or spiritual. My shadow, lengthening in the afternoon sun, walked beside me now, to my right along the Bedford road leading to Halifax, a mere five miles ahead on my southern course. And my shadow no longer led me–my companion now, I felt, one with whom I was in league, an ally, not a master. Other shadows appeared cast by barn, farmhouse and tree and mine was, from time to time, lost in these, indistinguishable from them in their common darkness, like the men who occupied the farms I passed.

The substantial world I discovered myself in was, it seemed, a shadow cast by the light of its creator which light is obscured, even obstructed, but the mind which forgets this light and lives, apparently, by a light of its own which is its shadow. The mind that is the circumstance when circumstance seems creative, in a world where possession is the sole refuge of the dispossessed. Looking ahead I saw the more prosperous-looking farms of Dutch Village, which reminded me of our own Lunenburg in the neatness of its houses and gardens as well as the brightness of its gaily-painted buildings. The city was still a mile or two ahead to the south-east behind a hill whose western slope glowed gold in the setting sun. Skirting the tip of the NorthWest Arm the road that I followed led up the hill, my shadow agreeing to lead the way up its steep slope. The Arm lay encased in shadow and light, dark in itself, the dividing waters between the shadowed eastern slope and the sun-illumined western hill we now climbed, through meadows cleared of obstructing brush, adorned by trees the farmers had left for shade or future firewood. Our road was easy now, free of rocks and boulders, grateful to the traveller's weary feet. He and his fellows here had long forgotten their apparent victory over tree and stone, the dispossessed whose darkness was the light of survival and whose light was a fortress against growth, living by the alliance of dark and light but choosing to see only light in their darkness. We reached the summit of the hill and looked toward the darkened slope where the city lay before our eyes. There were shadowy dwellings, phantom fields and public buildings, crowned by Fort George whose elevation let the fortress catch the last rays of the setting sun, the fortress's walls a brilliant gold, a jewel resting in the dark setting. Beside and behind it where lights began to appear in darkened houses like echoes of the greater light under whose wing they flourished. Before me, my shadow lengthened infinitely now, his darkness stretching forward to be engulfed in a blackness like his own and providing a bridge-like path into the city I had walked so far to find, and into the court which we both sought so fervently. And within that city were the prisoners, shadowy now, awaiting the light to come, sitting in their darkening jail cells, shade within encroaching shade.

We continued on, passing beneath the walls of the fortress and thinking of those within it. Soldiers under Law, sworn to uphold and defend that Law against all its enemies, foreign and domestic; and within other walls, not far distant, walls that arose with the fortress walls, the fortress of Law and the prison, its shadow. The North West Arm road turned into Sackville Street. We followed it eastward down into a darkness like that of a mine shaft or a ship's hold only relieved here and there by a dim light from a distant shelter. In this darkness we became one; we could no longer be distinguished one from the other. Although I knew him to be present, and therefore separate from me, my eyes showed me nothing but blackness, the colour we shared now, crossing Barrack Street. At the crossing we were at a point half-way between the fortress over our left shoulder and the jail forward of our right–two enclosures, one shadowing forth the other, but, in their effect upon those within, indistinguishable, much like my shadow and I, the judged and the judge.

I saw two men in one; I had come to this first in contemplating what little I saw of the *Saladin* case through newspapers. This puzzling twoness and the need to resolve it drove me to walk to our capital; on the journey I found the sense of twoness growing, reaching its height on the stony mountain at St. Margaret's head. And it continued, as it still does now in recounting it after arraignment, trial, sentence and return, there in the streets of the capital where we–or rather I–sought and at last found a modest boarding house, the Harbour Light, at the corner of Forman's Division and Buckingham.

Perhaps the best device I might use to clarify my sense of twoness would be to realise myself in the form of Captain Cunningham, Abraham Cunningham from Antigonish, the one who first boarded the *Saladin* at Harbour Island. In his experience I see my own and, therefore, if experience in common makes the men who live through it alike, I am Cunningham; he, in this realisation, is my eyes. Let it be so, for in this I am only granting myself a reprieve for violating the revenue laws of identity; customs demand its pound of flesh, I know. Losing my ship because of this infraction only makes me a passenger on another; the loss is only an apparent one under whatever authority I may live. My ship, the two-masted schooner *Artemis*, was singled up at the dock at Drumhead, Country Harbour. A sou'easter brought scattered mist, heavy mist, heavy seas and twenty-five knot winds; the voyage to Halifax would be rough and slower than I had hoped. Speaking trumpet in hand, I was about to give the order which would free us from the land when two shore people appeared on the deck calling on me to wait; they had news of importance. It seemed a barque under full sail had run aground on a reef at the southern tip of Harbour Island. Such seamanship appalled me; I remember I immediately suspected that all could not have been as it should be on such a ship, being, as I am, quick to judge and to condemn in such matters. I swear as a god-fearing man, taut seamanship is disappearing from these waters. Strict command and ready obedience are the key to seaman-like ship handling; but the barque needed help, and I got underway at once, soon leaving Drumhead and Country Harbour astern.

A long reach on the starboard tack brought the *Artemis* to a bearing directly between Beach Point on Goose Island and Burke Point on Harbour Island. Heading south, then, we proceeded toward the southern tip of Harbour Island, a mile ahead, still hidden by fog patches and heavy seas. I peered ahead, straining my eyes to catch a glimpse of the unfortunate ship, but without success. I quickly confirmed the course, my eye on the foresail that had begun to luff, when a voice from forward shouted, "There she is, sir, two points off the starboard bow!" There in the mist and surf, eight hundred yards ahead, was the wrecked ship, barely distinguishable in the fog, rolling from side to side. As she rolled, her bow in the midst of boiling surf as far aft as her forechains, she groaned–yes, it was her death agony, long and shattering, which she suffered under full sail, wind driving her forward, reef obstructing that forward driving force, and she was being crushed between them. As we sailed closer I could distinguish her rigging, the long boat to starboard, and some men, shadowy figures, running frenziedly fore and aft waving and calling, as phantoms do, in silent voices. My ship was within three hundred yards of the wreck now; I ordered the helmsman to bring her into the wind to lie to. I heard a voice from her bow; there was a man at her bowsprit, standing on her martingale guys and holding on to the dolphin striker with his left arm. In his right was a speaking trumpet through which he tried to make himself heard above surf and wind and grinding hull. "For God's sake, save us!" "What ship are you?" "Save us!" was all I heard. The boat was quickly lowered; my duty was clear. Heavy seas notwithstanding, I must board her and save her distressed crew.

My boat finally drew abreast of her to starboard, thirty yards away. A monkey-fist carried the line she passed over my bow; I bound it around my chest in a running bowline under my armpits, gave a signal to haul away and jumped into the surf. Striking out with my arms, I did the best I could to aid the men who pulled me toward them, my saviours under the immediate circumstances. As she rolled to starboard, they pulled me up, my feet struggling up the slippery hull amidships. On a level, at last, with the bulwarks, I grasped an extended hand and swung one leg over and then the other, landing on the deck alongside the galley. My immediate rescuers are two men, one a red-haired Englishman named Johnston, and the other a piratical-looking, black-haired man named Hazleton. Both were clearly drunk and frightened. "Welcome aboard, Captain," Johnston said, "the *Saladin* needs you if we're to survive at all." Behind them on the heaving deck, leaning against the galley for support, stood the other four members of the crew. No captain or officers were in evidence. I was both mystified and suspicious. Soaked as I was, however, I was grateful for their pulling me out of the sea– and strangely, I felt I was an invader, an interloper, even a pirate thus boarding another man's command; but there was no other man, no commander. Among the six men standing before me, four, including my recent rescuers, were clearly drunk. The other two seemed different from their shipmates; subservient to them, they yet manifested a separateness that caused me to turn to the eldest of them, one Carr, the cook, for information. He it was who had asked particularly that I be brought on board. "Too much rum has been drunk, sir; you can see for yourself its result. I thank God we have a captain again." His words proved him a God-fearing man whatever else he might have been. Then Johnston interrupted him, asserting his claim to command, but his blood-shot eyes and thick tongue belied the dignity he tried to establish; Hazleton, this drunken man's first mate, if the ravings of his commanding officer were to be believed, tried to support Johnston's assertion. "Since you beg to be saved," I said, "I am here to carry out your request; you are, by your fear for your lives, under my authority."

Even a teacher like myself can take command at sea to save an alien crew and even himself from death or indecision. At any rate the six, ruled by their fear, acknowledged my right. The heavy rolling continued and the seas broke over the poop from time to time; further delay invited disaster. If the wind shifted, the *Saladin* might slide astern into deep water where she would be certain to sink like lead. I turned to the task at hand, leaving the mysterious conditions she and her crew manifested unexplained in my desire to save her, or at least keep her on the reef long enough to allow our escape. Being her commander linked me to my unworthy crew in our subjection to a common danger. They obeyed me readily enough, however, and made short work of striking her canvas. The light sails were clewed up, and the ship's rolling eased off appreciably. This left me free to pursue my inquiries.

At my demand, Johnston, the others huddled around him, told their tale. The captain of the *Saladin* had died two months ago and his first officer three days later. The difficulty in shifting sail in bad weather had brought about the second officer's death; he had fallen overboard from aloft. The others had died in similar accidents. Out of fourteen, only six remained. The others affirmed the truth of his story. As I listened, straining to hear him above seas and the groaning of the ship, I chanced to glance at the deck starboard of the galley where I had first come aboard. Dark irregular stains on an otherwise holy-stoned deck were perhaps not unusual after so long at sea, but they puzzled me nonetheless. Johnston's drunken narrative was hardly convincing; as a witness his testimony seemed suspect, too much, how shall I say, up in the air, too far from safe ground. He seemed to gain strength as his tale continued, as if he fed on it, red head nodding decisively to emphasise each point. He and his three companions in drink had joined the ship in Valparaiso. She was headed for London with a valuable cargo and two passengers, both of whom were lost overboard rounding Cape Horn. Later, death having robbed them of their captain, Johnston had taken charge. Galloway, the steward, the man who I had seen as set apart from these with Carr, the cook, had a rudimentary knowledge of navigation. They had headed for the Gulf of St. Lawrence; six weeks later, just an hour before I came on board, she ran aground. Navigation without a captain, sailing without competent knowledge, was horrifying to me. The man's blind boldness was well nigh criminal; but, I asked myself, what could he have done? Survival is the Law at sea as elsewhere; it is the rock, the treasure, the cargo upon which a seaman's efforts are founded. It unites a body of men onto a single force bent upon reaching port. They had, but their port was a reef and their single force was spirit, but from a bottle. I condemned them in my mind, and ordered Johnston to take me to the cabin.

The stain I had seen forward reappeared on the quarter-deck as I descended the companionway into a chaos of clothes, nautical instruments, ship's papers and a chest of golden Mexican dollars filled to the brim. Sheltered from the weather, I looked around me to see a richly panelled main cabin, dark oak, reflecting the chaos on deck and table as well as my figure and Johnston's. An empty rum bottle rolled slowly across the deck, back and forth as the ship rolled, making a disturbing hollow sound in effect like this self-styled capin tain's tale. Sending for Carr and Galloway, I set them the task of putting the cabin's contents in order and making a inventory of them while the other three were set to salvaging what they could topside. My feeling an interloper, first experienced on the weather deck, intensified here. The activity topside had caused me to forget what now returned. What kind of a command was this? What had actually happened aboard the *Saladin*? The log, which I found in the after cabin, showed its last entry had been made at noon on April 13th, two degrees south of the Line. A boy's cap, under the chart table, I put in my pocket, as I did a locket containing a likeness of a woman. I found it on the lower bunk in a starboard stateroom. My earlier vague uneasiness began to change into conscious suspicion. The magnificent ship hid a succession of events I feared to guess, but felt compelled to investigate. The arms locker under the liquor cabinet was empty. Johnston said they had thrown them overboard fearing that they might be a temptation during their drunken brawling to which the chaotic cabin gave silent witness. I felt a vague fear of him, this man whose life I had come to save, and I saw a like fear of me in him. His rum-reddened, sleepless eyes were surly and defiant, but I was his rescuer. I must have seemed a ghost from another world to him as I stood there, in the main cabin once more, questioning him with eye and voice. He saw the Law before him, perhaps, in all its threatening ambiguity, but he defied it still, the defiance giving witness to his strength and the strength of what he feared.

On deck once more, I hailed my boat and sent it back to the *Artemis* instructing my first mate to return in her to Drumhead. Once there, he was to invite Charles Archibald, a Justice of the Peace, to return in the *Artemis* to the *Saladin*. It was with some misgiving that I watched her fade into the mist to starboard, my hands resting on the top of the hencoop. She disappeared and I looked down to see a third stain

the pine under my fingers; in the midst of this stain was a deep cut in the wood clearly made by an axe-blade. Puzzled and increasingly suspicious, I turned to find Johnston close behind me looking at the cut and stain. He stepped back as I turned, attempting to conceal what appeared as fear in his eyes. These men, I now know, were no longer my crew; they were my prisoners, I their jailer. The *Saladin*, a ship no longer, became a jail. And the key I possessed to the now safely locked liquor cabinet was my means to keep them under some vestige of control. The other means was to keep my secret. They did not know I was their jailer, and my discovery must be like my concealment, undiscovered as yet for our mutual safety. Our survival depended, apparently, on our ignorance, whether pretended or actual. The land, hidden now in the gathering darkness, ground away at the slowly shifting bow of the *Saladin*, just as my message to Archibald, ashore, was wearing away at the hidden secret of Johnston and his compatriots. The land and the Law were my source of safety; strange words from a sea captain, aren't they?

My possession of the ship, despite the concealed fears I felt, went undisputed. Johnston and his men saw their only hope in my authority; as long as their secret was kept they felt, in my presence, reasonably safe. Night fell; out of deference to me, or the need to confer in private, all six men went forward to sleep in the forecastle. I remained aft using the former captain's after cabin as a refuge. Seeking to clear some of the ship's thorny recent history, I once again consulted the ship's log and her papers. Her dead commander's name was Isaac MacKenzie; her complement included two passengers, one Captain Jacob Fielding and his son. The cap I had found and put in my pocket must have been the boy's. So I had inherited a wrecked ship which before this disaster had two captains–an unusual situation, certainly, but not unheard of. In a way, I was her fourth captain, being preceded by two dead men and a drunken sailor. In the dim light of the lamp over the chart table, with the moderating seas crashing regularly against the stern windows before my eyes and causing the ship to shift grindingly in the uneasy resting place she had found, I felt enclosed by shadows, by ghosts who were trying to speak, to tell, to warn me. The security of life under the clarity of the Law of the sea seemed threatened by the unspoken mystery I had come upon.

From the former certitude I had lived by, I had come to another perspective that put all in disturbing doubt. That MacKenzie and Fielding were dead I had no doubt, but how had they died? My questionings, my doubts, mutinied against the command of myself and the ship I possessed, but seemed to be losing at the same time. A valuable cargo is a great temptation; "For where your treasure is, there will your heart be also,"–the Sermon on the Mount, our Lord's words in Matthew's voice came to me. My treasure was command, and so, rising to my feet, I brought my fist down hard on the chart before me in the circle of light; "And, by God, I'll keep it, mutiny or no mutiny!" Something granular on the chart's surface stuck to my fist; inspecting it under the lamp I found some black grains which, when tasted, proved to be gunpowder. Dark stains, axe-blade cuts, an empty arms locker, gunpowder and empty rum bottles spoke to me in the dimness as I lay down to sleep after having made sure the cabin door was safely locked. I slept rocking uneasily to the sound of rushing seas and groaning hull. The last sound I heard was a voice apparently coming from astern: "Murder–murder," was all it said.

The following morning the weather cleared, and the seas moderated. After downing some of Carr's respectable porridge, I called the six aft. The *Saladin*'s running gear, as much as could be salvaged, was collected on deck prepared for offloading. This task completed, I sent all six men aloft to cut the sails from the yards and to remove as much of her running rigging as they could manage. The cargo was next. The guano in forward and after holds, valuable as it was, was left. The pigs of copper and silver I once again inventoried and had stacked on deck. The chest of Mexican dollars I counted– $10,000 worth, a noble treasure–joined the nautical instruments, the ship's compass and chronometers, and clothing amidships aft, between the two steerage hatches. They put the long boat over the side ready to launch just as Carr called my attention to an approaching schooner, soon identified as the *Artemis*. My command was a welcome sight; she was accompanied by the sloop *Apollo*.

Mr. Archibald was soon standing beside me on the quarterdeck. His air of authority and his self-possession restored my spirits. After a brief accounting for gear and cargo, I consigned the bills of lading and exchange, indentures and the ship's papers and log to the magistrate. I also gave him a full account of my short command aboard the *Saladin*, voicing my suspicions and showing him what evidence I could. He shared my suspicions. The six men, the cargo, and the valuables were put under his charge, gratefully out of my possession and into the hands of the Law. The magistrate and two men together with the valuable cargo returned to Drumhead in the *Apollo*; the remainder followed in the long boat. I watched the two vessels from the quarterdeck of the *Saladin*, the wreck sadly stripped and broken, hardly a command any longer. She had lived her life and now was dying, a lost soul being devoured by the rocks of Harbour Island. Harbour indeed! A grave is only a refuge, a safe harbour, for the dead– she had violated the Law of the sea whose sentence is as unlife, plete my task and return to the *Artemis*. The *Rosamond* was a tractable, swift craft and the voyage, I thanked God, was soon over. Rounding Cape Mocodome on a north easterly course, we approached Country Harbour in the early evening to see the shadowy *Saladin*, stripped and on her beam ends, looking more corpse-like than I had remembered. Her hull was now

moving and hard as rock itself, and whose verdict is ever as sudden as its execution is slow. My boat waited; I descended to it over the stern to starboard. As the crew pulled toward the *Artemis*, the *Saladin*, already heeled over to starboard, suddenly lifted as if trying to float free and, with a rending groan, went over on her beam ends. It seemed I was well free of her and her tale; my command lived in the *Artemis* as it, in a sense, had died in the *Saladin*. Separated as I was from the wreck and standing once again on my own deck, I felt the exhilaration that a condemned man must feel at the news of a last minute reprieve. And that reprieve could only come by perdition to the Admiral at Halifax to bring the six prisoners in Archibald's charge to justice. Only through Law could they survive, the Law of the sea embodied in Admiralty Court, which would return them to the state of men, seamen, the state they had defied, the Harbour Island to which their faulty navigation had brought them.

The voyage to Halifax was uneventful. I reported to the Admiral on Saturday, the 25th, requesting that a ship be dispatched to Drumhead to bring back the valuable cargo and the six men. The Admiral's headquarters, shipshape and suitably grand, seemed a refuge to me, a retreat where protection and comfort joined, free from storms of doubt and the rocks and shoals of fear. It was the home of Law in which I stood. The man seated before me in the brilliant blue and gold of his naval uniform, suggesting as it did the sea with the sun upon it, and the readiness with which he acceded to my urgent request, all combined to give me renewed strength and firmness of purpose. My fears died a natural death, it seemed, in those surroundings; my inner sense of command, shaken so recently, regained its former predominance. On the wall behind the Admiral, I noticed, hung a handsome reproduction of the well-known painting depicting the death of Nelson on the decks of *H.M.S. Victory*. My pride as a seaman was enhanced by the knowledge that I, too, shared, in my sea-going the life of the naval hero. The Admiral's voice recalled me to myself, saying that he would dispatch the schooner *H.M.S. Fair Rosamond* to Country Harbour in company with two sloops to bring what was left from the *Saladin* to the capital. I was ordered to sail in the *Rosamond* accompanied by a Mr. Michael Tobe, a Lloyd's agent, to Country Harbour to supervise the collection and return of men and cargo to Halifax. This was somehow disconcerting, although I concealed my misgivings from my superior. I had no wish to see the *Saladin* or her crew again; my sense of emancipation was thus shadowed, but the voice that commanded me must be obeyed. I thanked the Admiral for his readiness to listen and turned to go. Two marines in their red uniforms stood at the door; as the afternoon sun shone through a western window, the two men seemed like twin flames guarding the door to a Hades I had not chosen but into which I was forced to go. One flame bent to open and then closed the door behind me. I had crossed the Line and now, with slow steps, began the return journey to Drumhead, bound by the orders I had received, losing by them my ship, however temporarily, and my command. The task, I hoped, making me a mere passenger on the *Rosamond*, would soon be over. The delivery of the six men to the jail would be my delivery as well, my release from unwanted service.

The *Rosamond* got underway the next morning at daylight. Mr. Tobe and myself, the only passengers, got aboard and stood passively by watching the naval crew work their ship. I felt bound, robbed of my life; it seemed that the Admiral's willingness to fulfil my request while it was the treasure I sought, also deprived my of my life–the conflict within was echoed in the heavy weather that eventually forced the ship back to port. The next day the elements were more propitious and we proceeded to Country Harbour without mishap. My inner conflict, however, was not allayed; it simply changed form to become well nigh ungovernable impatience to com-

breached in several places and the guano she carried had leaked out and coloured the sea around her in a shroud of pale, luminous whiteness, a ghostly and chilling sight. She seemed to have died before her death, hanging desperately to the rocks which devoured her for a safety that could only end by destroying her completely. I watched her from the quarterdeck, my thoughts crowding one upon another as I recognised in her as she now was the image of my command and the life it held for me–yes, the image–or the shadow. Robbed of her stern windows, figurehead and name by rapacious salvagers, the seas now rolled freely through her cabins and holds. The sea she once floated so proudly upon had entered her, had engulfed her within and without; as the rocks had devoured her hull with their teeth, so now I saw the sea swallow her–she drowned, sliding into the waters and so lost to my sight forever, hidden in the ocean's maw. All that remained as we left her site on the reef off our starboard quarter was the luminous shroud that marked her grave. I choked, a lump in my throat; what had I lost? It was the shadow of death I had seen; the sea had taken it. I suddenly felt a freedom I had never previously known. My shadow was gone; I survived and lived on; only the consciousness of her remained, the other watch from which I would not escape–but this doubleness did not seem to confine, but quite the opposite.

The *Rosamond* docked at Drumhead as night fell. I dined at the Drumhead Inn with Mr. Archibald, Mr. Tobe and Lieutenant Eden, Captain of the *Rosamond*. My duty and my eagerness to meet the exigencies of the task before me turned our meal into a drumhead court; the six men were quickly condemned to be returned as prisoners to Halifax. The arrangements for transporting them and the valuable cargo in the *Rosamond* were concluded and the two sloops that had accompanied us were to transport the copper bits and salvaged gear to the capital within the week. But Archibald brought some news that angered as much as frightened me. It seems the six men had been confined in a nearby barn under watch day and night by a series of volunteer guards he had enlisted as soon as the *Apollo* had docked. Two nights before, one Jonah Freeman had fallen asleep while on watch, and the six had found him, bound him hand and foot, and escaped. My faith in Mr. Archibald was ill-founded, it seemed, and I immediately demanded a search party from Eden's crew to be gathered and sent after them. This was quickly executed, a boatswain and six men, well armed and led by Freeman himself, who knew the country, disappeared into the night. My prayers for their safe and successful return went with them.

At dawn the next day, nothing had been heard from the search party. My anxiety was allayed somewhat by the demands of loading the ships and turning over the papers signifying possession to Lieutenant Eden. By noon the loading was completed. I was standing at the dockside performing a final accounting of the cargo when the party returned, their prisoners in irons, accompanied by a gentleman from Halifax who had been sent overland to apprehend and take into custody this last vestige of the ghostly *Saladin*. He had discovered them with the aid of a local farmer about ten miles from Country Harbour, hungry and hopelessly lost. Joined by the search party at dawn, the men returned to Drumhead as quickly as the stony terrain and crudely fashioned road would allow. To my eyes, the prisoners were no longer men; like the *Saladin*, the Law had swallowed them–they were shadows, spectres whose life, reminding me again of what the sinking *Saladin* had made me conscious of, seemed already closed. Yet they were standing before me still, dead before he turned over to the authorities, leaving the *Saladin* where she lay on the rocks of the island that resolution seems to place at every harbour mouth in a country of safety. But given this wreck and salvage, what of the survivors? What of the men who had sailed in her, had given their lives in her service? Hadn't I served on her also, even before as after her demise?

the sentence was passed which was their only refuge, the sentence which would make them men again. I ordered them stowed below in irons; as they descended only Johnston turned back to look me in the eye. He raised his right arm, manacled as it was, touched his forelock in a mock salute: "The *Saladin* may be gone, but I'm not–not yet, by God," he said as he disappeared.

How nearly Cunningham and I are cousins german! Indeed more than cousins, perhaps, even the same man with the same eyes. Well, the *Rosamond* brought the prisoners and treasure to the capital just as the *Saladin*'s case brought me. My legs and the naval sloop being far from unlike as we might suppose from their outward form. Captain Cunningham and I needed that Admiralty Court, for it alone could resolve the dilemma; paralysing as it seemed, yet driving us to an activity far beyond the deadly limits of that fatal disease. It seems to me, however, that an Admiralty Court and execution make a poor cure for paralysis; I shall see, however, God willing.

CHAPTER THREE

The Exchange

You were upon the trackless deep, with all the world before you.
The Sentence.

The Golden Inn, Lunenburg, 8 August, 1844: The meeting the *Saladin* case brought about for me also imprisoned me, giving rise to a sense of confinement that still oppresses me as I continue to tell of it. But meetings change circumstances, introducing different perspectives; the coin of righteousness that I hoarded so jealously came to me at a price: the four hanged men and two survivors reduced my capital without hope of restitution. I had lost, and the Law was the thief, nay, the pirate. I had run ashore under full sail, suffered the rigours of shipwreck, driven over on my beam ends by wind and tide. And I visited the wreck, as I do now once again as an unseen witness. I must watch to see if I proceed with the circumspection and the detachment self-evaluation demands. This meeting, I notice, has a third observer, as every meeting must. The stranger I met on the *Saladin*, whether I wanted to or not, became, along with me in our confining relationship, the originator of the investigator as well. Three, I come to see, is an even number. The investigator viewed the wreckage, looked over Bills of Lading, cargo, clothing, and stores and saw the paraphenalia of sea-going ventures. This

My search for profit, for treasure, for security through the re-establishment of the rectitude of the view I had, and still have, perhaps, of the human condition required all my faculties, my self, in all its various forms, to serve this one purpose.

Sailing under the auspices of moral winds upon natural seas, which threaten a ship and give her passage simultane-ously, I engaged in the commerce of government, of order, of economy in the full sense. At sea, apparent success, while the land, the island brought disaster, confiscation, confinement through an infraction of the Revenue Laws. The self, or selves, that served at sea became prisoners. They seemed, and still seem, the victims of what looms as my moral counting house, enlisted under my authority to serve, to survive, perhaps. But what is survival worth when it is seen only in food and drink, the preparation and serving of the meat that gives us what we choose to nominate life? And what authority is strong enough to take this view from us, to rob us of this survival, the foun-dation? Desire to survive seems to make us, to create us, to bring us life, if it is living to be enslaved thus to the services of cook and steward. The dilemma is unresolved; does this condemn me? Midas's gold is merely his desire for authority transformed to a tangible object, the last but hardly the least of which was his daughter. So I shall continue the transform-ing, the telling in and by which I can perhaps find what I seek so fervently to possess, even if it means usurping the author-ity I have freely learned to serve, living, perhaps, by imagin-ing what may have occurred or is occurring.

At sea off the west coast of Chile, 22 February, 1844: Since the *Saladin* left Valparaiso in her wake on 8 February, the weather had been favourable to the ship's progress south, uneventful to all appearances. Captain MacKenzie's command was apparently secure. The crew haunted their stations on watch, shifting sail as wind and mate required, and off watch pursued their duties, their eating and their sleeping like will-ing servants whose existence seemed the gift of the captain they obeyed. He, in turn, served the elements that made him captain and exacted his obedience in return for the security which authority seeks. Captain MacKenzie, at sea, lord of the creation. His dominion brought to life found, he thought, deferential and even willing servants in the ghosts who obeyed him. The one discord in an otherwise undisturbed dream was his two passengers, the father and the son.

From their meeting in "The Sign of the Trap" in Valparaiso, through the early days of the voyage, MacKenzie's initial sharing in Captain Fielding's strong sense of the life of authority continued to exert its force. Captain MacKenzie felt it as he felt his ship pitch and roll under him, forcing its way south through seas which seemed bent upon obstructing its wind-driven forward motion. But now the presence of his passenger-partner's sense of authority began to disturb the captain. This feeling showed itself in Fielding's actions. He began by asking to see the *Saladin*'s Bill of Lading. Informed of her cargo and its market value, he next pursued inquiries about officers and crew, seeking to learn their origins, breadth of experience and character. He stood no watches, but spent long hours on the poop deck, observing the *Saladin*'s sailing qualities and overseeing the watch-standers. His relationship with the crew, perhaps, disturbed Captain MacKenzie the most. Fielding, while he had no official authority on the ship, found occasion to order the crew about in small matters, commanding them to secure Irish pennants, trim sails more efficiently, hold the *Saladin* on course with greater accuracy. This alone was irritating to captain, mate and crew, but the whose ghostliness embodied the reality of MacKenzie's authority, his treasure, his life.

The watch was relieved at noon, and its three members carried additional dissatisfaction to the forecastle. While it was only one incident among many, these men united in their sense of what had occurred. They began by cursing MacKenzie for his harshness and violence. But more significant because

ery with which his commands were delivered aggravated the injury to morale. His mocking tone and attitude insinuated the difference between the man addressed and the crewman who carried out his command, making the man seem less than he was while the sailor's competence was questioned. It was as if the man was seen as an obstacle to the efficiency of the sailor upon whom the safety of the ship precariously depended.

The forenoon watch was on deck, Anderson at the helm. His dark hair, swarthy skin and brown eyes seemed to belie his Swedish origin that his accent recalled. Fielding stood abaft the hencoop on the quarterdeck observing Anderson's helmsmanship. With a moderate following sea the ship yawed slightly. "Mind your course, helmsman, if that's what you are," Fielding said. Anderson remained silent, glancing angrily at the speaker; he attempted to correct his course, however, and in doing so swung past it by two points. At this moment Captain MacKenzie emerged from the companionway. He had heard Fielding's order. "I'll thank you to remember that you're a passenger on my ship. Keep your commands to yourself, Captain, while you sail with me. Anderson," he said, "you're off course–mind your helm, you land-lubber; I've had enough of your bloody carelessness!" With this he strode up to the helmsman and watched his attempts once again to correct his course. "Damn you, you've let her fall off again!" As he said this the Captain struck Anderson hard on the left shoulder, causing him to stumble and fall to his knees at Fielding's feet. Cursing under his breath, he regained his feet with Fielding's help and eventually took the helm again with a curse and a warning from Captain MacKenzie. "That's a cowardly way to handle a helmsman: you'll never train him by those methods, will you, Captain?" Fielding's mocking tone gave his insolence added sting. "Get below and hold your tongue, Captain. I won't have my command traduced by your interference." Captain Fielding, unperturbed, walked slowly to the mockcompanionway and, looking aft at the helmsman and Captain, smiled, gave a mock salute, and disappeared.

While this may appear to be a minor incident, it typified Fielding's constant behaviour, as it did Captain MacKenzie's growing animosity toward his passenger. It began to appear that what had brought about the Captain's accepting Fielding as a passenger, the latter's devotion to command, had now become a reason for wishing he had never met him. How could MacKenzie maintain essential ascendancy when a passenger was beginning to appear as a second Captain on board the *Saladin*? Anderson had obeyed Fielding's order, however reluctantly. MacKenzie's anger swelled within him; he longed for Fielding's absence. Waves of hatred swept him. Only long experience in self-control kept his feeling under some vestige of control. He gripped the taffrail with whitened knuckles and stared over the wastes of water that separated him from Valparaiso and the meeting with his passenger. He saw again Fielding's faintly patronising smile and mock salute as he had descended the companionway. Could he dismiss its ironic suggestion that his authority was subverted by his assertion of it? Why had he struck his helmsman? Fielding filled him with fear by forcing him to see in his own action the link between infraction and authority, and in this link his dependence, even slavery to the authority he worshipped. Fielding showed him his command in a new light; it was the helmsman, the crew, the ship that made him a captain, not the reverse. Circumstance became his creator; even less than Fielding, a mere passenger, was MacKenzie, now becoming the prisoner of his own self-condemnation. In gaining ascendancy, he had broken the Revenue Laws of the foreign country whose resources he coveted. The fear he felt within grew when he remembered that his action had been observed not only by Anderson, but also by Johnston and Hazleton–and the other members of the larboard watch, as well. His defeat showed in his having lain a hand on a man

of its uniqueness, they felt fear, not unrelated to their captain's. Not possessing his resources, they felt stirring within them the need to destroy their fear, to overcome it. The instinct for security had begun to rob them of the strength that subservience to Captain MacKenzie had given them. The order they knew as preservative had begun to threaten their sense of safety. The forecastle provided a thought-provoking reflection of the captain's cabin aft, and the *Saladin* sailed on driven by favouring winds and patronising seas, farther and farther south.

Fielding's response to the scene on the poop deck was to eat his noon meal in the cabin. A dark, heavy table athwartships surrounded by six chairs was the principal furniture of the space. A door in the after bulkhead led to the captain's sleeping quarters. Four doors, two in the larboard and two in the starboard bulkhead gave entrance to four small staterooms providing sleeping space for Byerby, the first mate, and for Fielding and his son. The companionway, forward, gave access to the poop deck above. Light and air came through a skylight provided with small hatches that could be opened in fair weather. The panelling in the cabin, like that wood of table and chairs, was of dark highly polished oak silently reflecting the occupants of the cabin. And, at night, the dim light of an overhead, gimbelled oil lamp. Fielding ate alone, being served his food by George Jones who had joined the *Saladin* in Valparaiso. The Irishman was swarthy with prominent blue eyes, a short, stocky figure, and a wooden stump from the knee down instead of a left leg that had been crushed by a falling spar in some earlier storm. He was one of those Irishmen who knew his rights; nonetheless, under Captain MacKenzie's orders, he agreed to act as steward until the *Saladin* rounded Cape Horn when he would take up his proper role as sail maker. Jones, in this dual capacity, looked after simple necessity for both ship and men. His wooden leg slowed him and brought Captain MacKenzie's abuse down on him for his inefficient clumsy service as steward. In the twelve days since the *Saladin* left Valparaiso, Jones had begun to resent his captain's abuse that he felt to be unjustified and which also aggravated his awkwardness by irritating an already highly strung temperament. Jones eagerly awaited Cape Horn and release from his stewardship.

Captain Fielding, observer of ship and crew as he was, had quickly grasped Jones's resentment and its source in his Irish pride. Frequent meetings between steward and passenger at meals had resulted in a patronising sympathy on the Captain's part and a meek subservience on the steward's. Jones had observed frequently recurring differences between MacKenzie and Fielding, the effect of which had recently been seen in Fielding's often absenting himself from the cabin at meal times. Jones's resentment found what he thought was an echo in Fielding's differences with the *Saladin*'s captain; he rather enjoyed the passenger's mocking tone when he addressed MacKenzie, envying Fielding's outrageous freedom from his captain's rigorous exercise of authority. Apparently MacKenzie was stalemated in this and could not control his passenger's powers of insubordination and insolence.

Jones served Fielding his food. Soon finished, the passenger addressed the steward as the latter began to mount the companionway, calling him back to sit for a time at the table. "MacKenzie and I are still at it, Jones; I find your captain, if a tyrant can be dignified with such a title, more violent as each day passes. I sometimes wonder how the owners can trust him with command of so valuable a cargo, knowing how der in the heavens, leaves its practitioners undisturbed in overlooking a fundamental distortion in order to enjoy the satisfaction of knowing where they are. Captain MacKenzie regained some degree of calmness by this means. He plotted the ship's noon position on the chart and, by dead reckoning, projected her course forward to determine when the *Saladin* should change her course to due east. The Carpenter, who

his damned abuse and violence can cause resentment. Perhaps they don't know how honest seamen take abuse; resentment brews anger, and anger feeds a man's need to act to defend his self-respect. A good sailor knows his rights."

Jones had listened to Fielding's talk before. He received the words silently, apparently unmoved except for his eyes. They brightened as he watched the speaker's face, hearing his own feelings made clearer through the words and the knowing tone and expression that accompanied them. "But Sandy's still the captain, ain't he? Nothing can change that, that I know of." One foot and then the other on the companionway steps silenced the speaker. Both men looked up to see Captain MacKenzie materialise before them. He gave no sign of having heard them, but he scowled at Jones who had just risen from his seat at the table. "Get those slops aft, and look lively, damn you!" The steward picked up the plate of scraps and an empty glass, proposing to move them to the galley. MacKenzie stood facing his steward with his back to Fielding. In pantomime, the passenger imitated a throat cutting with his hand clearly suggesting his sentiments toward MacKenzie. Jones, seeing the gesture, looked away, grinning, as Fielding rose and entered his stateroom without giving the captain the slightest sign that his presence was recognised.

MacKenzie then ordered his steward to bring his noon meal at once. While he was waiting, his passenger passed through the cabin and, as he mounted the companionway, turned to the man at the table. " I wish you good appetite," he said, "and may the taking of food remind you of your mortality as your authority apparently fails to do. Nothing short of shipwreck, mutiny or piracy could be expected to do that, could it? A disgruntled crew puts its commander on trial, now, doesn't it? And what verdict do you think would come down from your nine good men and true? Or do you even concern yourself with the resentment of ghosts–the men sacrificed at the windlass of authority. Mark my words!" MacKenzie, face flushed with anger, rose from his seat, shaking his fist at his passenger. "God damn your eyes," he shouted, " it serves me right for giving you free passage! Get out of my sight! I'll remind you that I'm in command on this ship." Fielding remained stationary at the foot of the companionway, staring defiantly at the speaker, who suddenly lunged toward him. "Lay a hand on me, and your command is no more," said the passenger, raising a defensive arm. MacKenzie grasped it roughly, intending to harm Fielding and steady himself as well. The force of forward motion and his weight drove Fielding up the ladder toward the quarterdeck; he was literally being raised to that confined commanding area by MacKenzie's powerful will. Their hostility, however, did not change their common devotion to authority, the will that united them; but Fielding spurned MacKenzie's shoulder with his foot as he climbed out of sight to the quarterdeck above them both. MacKenzie staggered back against the cabin table, regained his balance, and sat down apparently exhausted, temporarily overcome by the unmistakable sense of his partner's force of character which shook now, as it had before this, his certainty of the ascendancy he lived by.

Staring at the face reflected in the tabletop, he saw in his glass's circle on the table a ghostly, indistinct face and two dark eyes staring back at him; a surprising resemblance to Fielding struck him. He cringed before the image of what to him seemed death-like. Hearing Jones stumping down the ladder, he recovered, glanced at the tell-tale above him to assure himself that the *Saladin* proceeded on course, and, having been served his food, began to eat huge mouthfuls of pieces of hardtack floating like islands in a saline broth. Jones asked if he wanted more. "No, you damned lubber, I want nothing." Steward and food departed silently, and the Captain of the *Saladin* retired to the after cabin to complete from his observations of the noon sun the calculation of his position. Celestial navigation, based as it is on the hypothesis of precise or-

was also the second mate, would have the mid-watch on the morning of the 13th, a Saturday; he would instruct his mate to change course at 0330. All was well.

The intervening hours passed without overt incident. The angry turbulence within Captain MacKenzie's and Fielding's apparently differing inner feelings, shown outwardly as they had been on occasion, had spread to the forecastle and galley. The crew, sensitive to signs of weakening vigour in the exercise of authority by their Captain, began to growl like hunting dogs–dogs whose well being depends on obedience, but whose nature instinctively sees apparent weakness. Their Captain's physical violence revealed his authority transformed from vital detachment to snarling, animal-like reliance on muscle. He seemed to become more like them, and they felt in this a foreboding threat to their safety. In the stalemate between MacKenzie and Fielding they sensed the pangs of irresolution in their commander. This sensing of what seemed weakness they felt as fear, the same fear that any seaman feels at the thought of land unsought, a static shoreline that threatens his safety and his ship. There was a haunting fixity in the *Saladin's* inner state, fore and aft, brought to this condition by the outward rigidity of shipboard routine at sea, the man-made defense against the elements which serve his purposes and threaten his security. So the inner unrest remained hidden, controlled still by the violence that lies behind outward conformance to an order upon which survival seems to depend. The hours between the captain's calculation of his noon position and the time when the *Saladin* turned east passed without incident. The Carpenter headed the mid-watch, carefully followed his instructions. "Hard a-larboard, Jeremy; bring her head due east, make the coursc good!" A westerly wind and moderate sea granted the ship ease of response to the helmsman's ready obedience. Any apparent change seemed good, and now the *Saladin* was headed for the Atlantic and the port her servants sought, albeit Cape Horn, a six-day's sail ahead, lay between.

The quiet steady form of a ship at sea in moderate weather sometimes lulls those sailing in her into a pervading sense of security, much as her strength of construction images forth the supporting refuge of her government. But waking dreams of safety can, at sea, become nightmares. Moderate winds and sea sometimes transmogrify into gales and mountainous seas. If the ship's government founders, the ship alone cannot survive; if the ship founders, the crew may, with luck, reach some shore once foreseen as a threat but now eagerly embraced as a fostering mother. What, it may be asked, makes such monumental changes in inanimate circumstance whether man-made or God-made? Perhaps it is every man's desire to survive, his ideal, his *Diana*, the moon goddess, spied upon as she bathes, serenely naked, surrounded by her Naiads. The intruder's reward for his illicitly eyeing the goddess is her anger and swift punishment. So the eye punishes those who refuse to see the myth which lies before them.

Such a change engulfed the *Saladin* as she sailed eastward approaching Cape Horn. No storm beset her, but gale-force winds familiar in those latitudes accompanied by seas whose crests overshadowed her as she reluctantly struggled onward brought about a similar change in her complement. Suppressed rebelliousness was apparently forgotten in the face of threats from without. Traversing decks continually awash in seas that seemed to seek legitimate possession of the *Saladin* became a hazardous necessity. Safety lines ran from the forecastle aft to the ladders giving access to the poop deck and as *Actaeon*, from Peruvian soldiers. They had deprived him of his command, of his ship, of his sense of life, making him a mere passenger, a prisoner. Burning with anger at the recollection, he damned them again as they had damned him to the condition of a criminal, a slave. Sleep seemed now more ungraspable than when he lay down. His powers of recollection had brought him to a Tierra del Fuego of his own mak-

the captain's cabin. The officer-of-the-watch, grasping a starboard backstay, gave no orders. The roaring wind silenced him; he could only give unspoken encouragement to the helmsman lashed to the helm. Together with their ship, they found no respite from the onslaught of seas they could only dream of overcoming in their survival, submitting mockingly to a force that they, a few days before, regarded as complacently as a man whose success in breaking a stallion to the halter depends on the horse's ignorance of his enslavement. Exhausted by a watch's four-hour struggle, they were relieved by their tired shipmates. Seeking refuge in cabin or forecastle, they then attempted to feed themselves and to find respite in sleeping. They were there lashed in their bunks, until duty called them to bear witness, once again, to the strength of the elements which passed judgment on their folly and withheld what seemed a foregone verdict and sentence. Holds filled to the hatches with security were emptied by pirates and renegades who had run their ship aground on the island of apparent detachment. Only by rebellion could they regain possession of their ship. The *Saladin*, their Earth, had, it seemed, changed from a refuge to a trap; but how might a trap provide safety for free men? The question seemed to go unanswered as the witnesses to natural force, which had reduced them to mere spectres of vitality and strength, continued to guide the *Saladin* onward toward Cape Horn and the Atlantic.

In the after cabin, prevailing danger submerged the incipient threat to MacKenzie's authority that had surfaced in Fielding's calm but forceful insinuations. The conflict between the two men moderated to a truce under the force of elements outside the cabin; the possessor of authority, it appears, is no respecter of persons. Both men felt this and, like those in the forecastle, felt fear as well, fear that could only be alleviated by submission to the ship's demands upon them, met actively in MacKenzie's case, and passively in Fielding's. Fielding spent his time in his stateroom, isolating himself as completely he could. The defiance he had shown toward the captain of the *Saladin* continued, now showing itself in his absence in the face of present danger. Feeling contempt for MacKenzie's apparent lack of a firm grip on the authority his position demanded, feeling his own strength and love for command, his position on the *Saladin* as a passenger seemed degrading. His circumstances seemed to enforce passivity upon an unwilling, not to say undeserving, prisoner whose crime was his authority, whose infraction was his strength, and whose judge and condemner was a pirate who daily robbed him of the sense of authority he lived by. MacKenzie, ineffectual as he seemed, was confining him in the name of justice and discipline and, of all things, the survival of authority.

The *Saladin* was to pass south of Cape Horn the next morning, the 1st of March, at 0700. The night before, Fielding retired late, having consumed his ration of hardtack, salt pork and brandy well after the others had finished their meal. Rations having been reduced for the past four days because of the difficulty in preparing and eating them, the brandy inflamed the passenger to an unusual degree. His stateroom was dark as he fell into his bunk, lashed himself in as best he could, and prepared for sleep. The agonised creaking of the ship accompanied by the roaring wind and crashing seas that constantly engulfed his single porthole with black water and shadowy spindrift all but drowned any other sound. Sea boots stamping above his head gave infrequent signs that the watch was on deck. Fielding lay staring at the white overhead that gradually became dimly visible as his eyes accustomed themselves to the darkness. The sea water covering his porthole made him feel as if he were under water, drowning; the cabin increased this sensation in him, small and cell-like as it was.

His mind wandered in his sleeplessness to the dim whiteness of his tiny cell at the Convent at Pisco where his wounded shoulder had been cared for. It was the wound he suffered defending, however unsuccessfully, his command, the

ing; a Hades created by the "*non serviam*" in the service of which Fielding had lived. He repeated the sentence under his breath and saw himself on the darkened deck of the *Actaeon* anchored off Chincha, two pistols in hand, his second mate beside him. The wooden-legged Irishman who held his fowling piece cocked at what appeared to be soldiers swarmed over the bulwarks. Leading them toward the mizzenmast where the captain stood was a slight, ruddy-faced man with a grizzled beard and unnaturally piercing blue eyes–was it MacKenzie? A short struggle, shots exchanged, the burning pain of a wound revealed to his vision the dim whiteness of a Convent cell. Fiery sunlight, intense heat and seeming freedom of movement accompanied dark whisperings that led him to what seemed the whitewashed captain's cabin Fielding recognised as the *Actaeon*'s. But the portholes were heavily barred, and the companionway lacked its customary ladder. The cabin was a prison cell; flames enclosed it. More whisperings, a poncho to cover him, and he emerged from the burning cell, passed a sentinel who vaguely resembled MacKenzie once again, and hid himself in the ashes of the *Actaeon*. His ship, his command was no more. The flavour of brandy in what seemed a dark room shared with a stranger brought him once again to the dim whiteness of what could only be the *Actaeon*'s cabin; a red-headed Englishman named Trevaskiss, his first mate, stood before him.

Between them lay the shadowy form of a man wearing the clothing of a ship's commanding officer, his face hidden. "It's ours at last, Mister! I am now commander!" As he spoke these words, Fielding opened his eyes to the dim whiteness he seemed to have come from, *Actaeon* or *Saladin*? He repeated the word "commander," his waking voice a hollow echo in contrast to its former vital resonance. The sense of duality he had as he struggled to rise reverberating in him seemed strengthening and life-giving. "She's ours," he said aloud, echoing himself. He seemed confined to his bunk, unable to get to his feet. The lashings. He released himself and, putting his feet on deck, groped for his pocket watch. Seven ten. The *Saladin* was rounding Cape Horn at the tip of Tierra del Fuego. Fielding's waking dream had carried him beyond the Pacific into the Atlantic. It was time to act, the only known means of transforming idea into circumstance, dream into possession. The act and the possession were the same; the dream possessed him, and Fielding saw the *Saladin* in its true light. She was his; now to make it so. He would bring his crew to life, recalling them from ghostliness to vitality.

The father's voice stirred his fifteen-year old son from lethargy. Exhausted and pale from sleeplessness and the endless strain of staying on his feet during waking hours, he surveyed his father from the upper bunk with eyes widening in fear. The son looked as if he was seeing a ghost. "Show a leg, my boy; we've reached the Atlantic and all the world's before us." The son obeyed his ghostly father. Feet on deck, his features betrayed their origin: he was a smaller image of the man to whom he owed his life, and one who had paid this debt, if such it was, by having rescued his father from prison in Callao. He had provided the poncho under which Fielding had made good his escape. Captain MacKenzie's second passenger had, so far, imitated his father's contempt for their benefactor; the captain of the *Saladin* ignored his insolence. The crew, on the other hand, cultivated the boy's friendship. They found pleasure in talking with one who was beyond the reach of MacKenzie's Law, or seemed to be. They idolized him, turning him into something he was not, a free spirit, for their Fielding's ear as he gave an order, "Man the starboard topsail braces! Prepare to trim fore and main topsails!" The captain's command and the crew's response to it were simultaneous; Fielding saw before him the rhetoric of existing circumstances on the *Saladin*. They seemed to belie his vision; the *Saladin* seemed to show no signs of becoming the *Actaeon*. The Captain, unperturbed by this, fed quietly on his vision; the *Saladin*

own delight. The boy was on familiar terms with all of them by the time the *Saladin* reached the Atlantic. In particular, he shared the larboard watch's rebelliousness under MacKenzie's abuse.

Four day's sail brought the *Saladin* into more moderate seas and fresh winds no longer of gale force. On the 4th of March she headed north-east and sailed on toward the Line over four thousand miles away. The *Saladin* had weathered Cape Horn, but she had paid the price: torn sails, standing and running rigging showing signs of strain, a severely damaged long boat and decks heavily encrusted with corrosive salt, mute legacy of the encroaching seas–all required immediate attention. Warmer weather and the re-establishment of the familiar ship's routine found the crew willing to occupy the long days of early autumn making repairs. MacKenzie's Law prevailed, it seemed, and the *Saladin*'s complement acquiesced. Under the Law's rigour, severely tried as the crew had been by Cape Horn, they readily set to work repairing the damage done by wind and fear, by sea and defiance, by light rations and rebellious mutterings. Former grievance was forgotten in the eagerness for return to the security of sea-worthiness. They were possessed by a dream; now it remained only to make it so. Captain MacKenzie continued to abuse his men and their resentment remained, but it was submerged beneath the choppy surface of their urgent tasks. Fear sometimes seems assuaged by the very activity that manifests it, a driving force arising from the desire to survive. Their captain's abuse defied them, asserting their failure as men; their efforts to reconstruct his authority make them his servants, reiterating in action the very abuse they sullenly resented. Their obedience was his abuse; they were the ghostly arms and legs of a shadowy figure that gave life and apparent animation to the *Saladin*, the ship that carried them forward by the impersonal powers of wind and sea, fear and defiance.

MacKenzie's violence and abuse were his chosen tools,

the axe and maul he used to keep his authority seaworthy. His men were the material possessions with which he could not only perform repairs but also transform the damaged, the imperfect, into a seaworthy state. The men were both what was damaged and that which could repair it, long boat and axe-maul, sail and needle and threaded eye. Their ghostliness and his, their fear and his loomed large, for the Law under which they lived defied these men and in that defiance confirmed the lie they chose to survive by. If MacKenzie and his crew manifested a likeness that their actions materialized, who commanded them? Where was the detached, impersonal authority, where the man who served their wishes by his guidance? They had become the ghostly passengers on a ship whose present life had been theirs, but they had given up that life, preferring their seemingly spectral existence, passive figures whose vitality lay exclusively in submitting all to the vessel which carried them onward with fear-inspiring, patronising, illusory independence.

Fielding's former characteristics were seen in his passive exercise of authority, his insolence, his agonising under the apparent loss of command. The consequent reduction to a sense of isolation only a solitary passenger can know, showed signs of what I have described as a waking dream of rebirth, of a new sense of life. The *Saladin* had become the *Actaeon*, the lost was found; the passive passenger was now the active captain. Fielding surveyed his passengers from the quarterdeck. He stood there with his son beside him listening to the sounds of axe and maul as the Carpenter and Collins repaired the long boat just forward of the starboard steerage hatch in the shadow of the mizzen shrouds. MacKenzie, standing beside him, observed the helmsman and eyed the set of the sails. "Your rigorous exercise of command bears fruit, I see," said Captain Fielding, "the crew's ready acquiescence shows in the rapid and efficient repairs proceeding forward there." MacKenzie did not reply; his voice had a haunting quality to

was the *Actaeon* still. Captain Fielding felt the need to act to bring into being what he saw as already existing. How he would begin to make his passengers see their condition had been the subject of his waking thought since his words "She's ours" had awakened his son off Cape Horn. In his judgment Jones, the steward, would best serve his purpose. The wooden-legged Irishman's former resentment under MacKenzie's abuse hadn't abated; he was, at the least, a reluctant passenger on the *Saladin* which made him a useful member of the *Actaeon*'s crew in her captain's eyes. Formerly he had been the substitute steward who served Fielding his food in the after cabin. Since Galloway had become the steward at Cape Horn, he was now sail-maker who might serve Fielding headier nourishment, the link to help raise him to command. Jones was to become a safety line stretching from the after cabin to the forecastle.

Captain Fielding saw him as the unifying figure that had nourished the cabin and wielded strong influence in the forecastle; as sail-maker he was not required to stand watch. This made him an aristocrat among common folk. They listened to what he said. And Jones had an appetite for Fielding's as yet unspecified repast; the latter had seen this clearly enough in the grin he had brought to the sail-maker's face when he cut MacKenzie's throat, if only in pantomime. Now it remained to convince certain other passengers to join in the pantomime that would make the *Saladin* the *Actaeon*, transforming passive passengers to active crew. Jones, Captain Fielding decided, was his man.

On the afternoon of Wednesday, 13 March, Captain Fielding strode vigorously forward beside the larboard bulwarks. Sun, light airs, and moderate seas lent a mask of benevolence to the scene that was also extant in the ship and in the minds of her crew under MacKenzie's Law. To Fielding, however, the ship was a phantom manned by ghostly figures. He saw the standing and running rigging, the sails and spars and decks as ghostly configurations of MacKenzie's Law, waiting quietly and in apparent submissiveness the vital hand, the transubstantiating force of flesh and blood to give it life. Sitting on deck and using the foremast to support his back while repairing a torn topgallant foresail was Jones. Suddenly Fielding found himself standing over the sail-maker, who carefully and precisely stitched together two lengths of sail-cloth and a strengthening strip of patching with his blunt, heavy needle and stiff thread.

Fielding's shadow fell across Jones and his work; the sail-maker looked up; but the brightness of the afternoon sun turned his visitor into a dark shadow. Three bells sounded from aft–half past five; seeing Jones's squint, Captain Fielding stepped forward a pace. His shadow continued to cover the sail-maker, but he had made himself visible by his slight movement. Enveloped by the huge grey weathered sail as he was, Jones looked not unlike a body emerging from the formlessness of a previous ghostly condition. "So there you are, Captain," Jones said, "coming at me from out of the sun." "There's a matter that might make your sewing that misty sail cloth no more than a memory, George. There's a dragon to fight, and the sail's his; you're repairing it makes you his, a threat to your life," said the Captain. Jones's face showed his failure to grasp more than the spirit of the speaker's remark. "The sail is mine as much as it's his, it seems to me, Captain" he rejoined, " but what's this about a threat to my life?" Byerby's voice called from aft for Moffat, Collins, and Allen thing you must do is get word of this to the larboard watch. Johnston first, then Hazleton, then Anderson; with that watch behind us, the other can be easily dealt with." "Aye, aye, sir," said the latest condemned member of the *Actaeon*'s crew, Captain Fielding commanding. They parted while the *Saladin*'s rigging continued to whisper her protest under the stress of wind and sea.

to relieve the first dog watch. They passed Captain Fielding and Jones as they moved aft along the starboard side, preventing the Captain from replying; now the three were well aft, and Fielding answered. "This is no time for clarity. Meet me at the galley, port side, after the mid-watch has the ship. You'll see the difference between this death and another life, there. You will lose your life if you don't." As Captain Fielding spoke, he moved aft leaving in Jones both fear and curiosity; serving MacKenzie continually forced him to swallow his pride, his sense of what he called his rights, by the act of submitting. He felt deprived, but of what he did not know. He only sensed he was not MacKenzie's man. He would meet with the Captain, if only to satisfy his curiosity.

Darkness deepened by a starless night transformed the daylight solidity of the *Saladin* into a shadowy *Actaeon*. Only creaking blocks and whispering sails and intermittently groaning rigging told the mid-watch that the shadows they dimly saw had substance. A steady wind permitted the watch a respite from activity; they sprawled on deck using taffrail and hencoop to support their backs. The feeble light from the binnacle illuminated Allen's pale face from below, making it appear skull-like, eyes sunken in dark holes from which they glittered–the incarnation of a death's-head; the ship spoke to silent listeners, whose eyes the binnacle light made blind to the forward decks and forecastle. Even the companionway was invisible when a figure Byerby thought was his captain emerged and passed silently forward to disappear in the blackness. The first mate paid no heed to what his eyes revealed.

Captain Fielding moved confidently forward as if he could see in the dark. Arriving at the galley amidships to larboard, he stopped and waited, betraying no anxiety; he knew his man. Out of the darkness forward a form, only recognisable by its deeper blackness, appeared. To confirm another presence, both men reached out and touched the other's shoulder at the same time. Satisfied, they moved just forward of the galley, using it as a shield against the invisible watch behind them. Captain Fielding reminded Jones of their former exchanges about MacKenzie, their mutual mistrust of his assertion of authority ending with the latter's violent attack on the Captain at the companionway. The speaker cited MacKenzie's continuing abusiveness, his heavy drinking, and his present illusory confidence in the security of his command; he had apparently lost his eyes, even in his mind. The Captain proceeded like a prosecuting attorney to open his listener's eyes to the weakness of a command that relies on verbal and bodily violence for its force: MacKenzie also had forgotten he was an old man. And there was also the ship's cargo to consider: copper, silver and specie. "What a fine prize a pirate would make of it." But there was other treasure the captain sought to share with the sail-maker. Under such a man as MacKenzie their lives were in danger; "Now Jones, if you want to save your life, now is the time. I have spoken to the Carpenter, and I intend to be master of this ship."

An unaccountable source of light revealed Captain Fielding, upright and strong, a figure powerful and beyond the sail-maker's strength to resist, hesitate as he might; "You've made your case and I'm behind you, Captain," he said, "damn old Sandy anyhow!" As he said this, Jones felt the blood rush to his head; Captain Fielding, a voice out of the darkness, had indeed made his case. Jones was enthralled by evidence that came to life in his eyes. But as its force was felt, another sensation arose in him; he was both the accused and the judge before the bar of a Law court in which the judge passed sentence on himself, and lived again through the death-sentence he passed. Arraignment had brought him to trial where he confessed the force of the argument he had heard. He was to act on it in the name of survival. What he saw in it gained ascendancy over the seer. "I intend to be master of this ship;" the words re-echoed in his mind. He, Jones, was to find a new life in taking part in his captain's plan. "Good man. The first

As Fielding moved aft he knew the elation, the sense of vital strength that accompanies the transformation of a dream into substance, into circumstance. Jones was his slave to do with as he pleased. It mattered little to the commander of the *Actaeon* that he made men into spectres to serve his aims. The authority he sought so fervently and the man who sought it were one; he was the Law. Having nearly reached the break of the poop at this point, the Captain tripped and stumbled over an unseen obstacle, the starboard steerage hatch. He caught a mizzen shroud and kept himself from falling to the deck. Recovering his balance, Fielding smiled to himself; yes, the phantom *Saladin* was his means to salvation, just as his servant Jones would bring that salvation about. Suddenly a sense of condemnation, of a kind of death engulfed him; he was sinking, unable to move his arms or legs to save himself. He was trapped; his means to survive was to finish what he had begun. Yes, finish. Dogged resolution restored, it seemed, the Captain's strength and had left his fear to fend for itself. The taste of command, savoured in Jones's ready capitulation, nourished Fielding and his growing dream. He reached his stateroom and lay in his bunk, prevented from sleeping by the accusing pain in his left leg; that damned steerage hatch!

Favourable winds and weather for the following three weeks brought the *Saladin* on her northeasterly course closer and closer to the Line. MacKenzie's confident voice, his passivity before the illusion of security in command, continued during this period, as did his habitual abusiveness. Captain Fielding's patronising words seemed to the *Saladin*'s commander a welcome change from the former's previous ironic hostility. This new harmony between the two men reminded MacKenzie of their first meeting at "The Sign of the Trap" in Valparaiso. He still felt the weight of his passenger's authoritative air, but he felt fear no longer; it seemed that Captain Fielding had modified or at least found a means to suppress his hostility. All seemed well. It was during this period that

Jones, Captain Fielding's bailiff, brought the three men the captain cited to judgment. The galley provided a suitable court room, and a succession of mid-watch meetings took place as MacKenzie's spectres chose to become Fielding's incarnate servants. Resentful spectres, it seemed, felt their flesh and blood protesting its innocence before the sentence handed down from the quarterdeck condemning them to hard labour in the *Saladin* for life. Captain Fielding's voice, heard in the midnight whisperings of Jones, sounded to their ears like the voice of an advocate defending them against an unjust fate. Their advocate would free them, and freedom would not be their only reward. The freedom would be materialized in money and survival. No longer would they risk their lives under a hard but feeble master whose authority rested in curses and blows.

Johnston was Jones's first captive. Twenty-three years old, ten of which had been spent before the mast, made him the most experienced seaman among the crew. He had joined the ship in Valparaiso having deserted from the *U.S.S. Constellation* there. He, like Captain Fielding, sought passage to England, his homeland. Six feet tall, muscular, with red hair, he had the bold air of one who maintained his difference from other men by his strength of arm and indifference to external controls. His self-possession was without limit; hence he signed on the *Saladin* under an assumed name. As MacKenzie's spectre he was known as Johnston; in Captain Fielding's command his name was Trevaskiss. Not unlike the *Actaeon*'s captain, he found being two men a useful device, the four to judgment and the sentence in each case had been life. On the 10th of April, only 300 miles south of the Line, the opportunity arose.

William Carr, the ship's cook, was taken ill on Wednesday, April 10th. The middle-aged widower, with two children in London in his elder sister's care, was nervous and devout.

but only a device which permitted him the illusion of self-possession sometimes enjoyed by the dispossessed. In telling Johnston of Captain Fielding's case, Jones found him ready to listen but disconcertingly silent. In the darkness of the galley, Jones's brief rested on the threat to his listener's life if he refused to join his captain. Others knew of the case, and if Johnston didn't agree, the others would kill him. The Englishman sneered at Jones's argument; he felt no fear for himself. Then Jones reminded him of the richness of the *Saladin*'s cargo; Johnston began to waver. His share in the cargo would make him into the man he thought himself to be. He was, it seemed, a servant of Captain Fielding. "I'll go for my share," he told Jones, and they parted, two created embodiments of a single master. If MacKenzie had two mates to serve him, so did Captain Fielding—the *Actaeon*'s crew now had its complement of officers, albeit at the forecastle's expense.

Later the midnight galley was the scene of another judgment. Hazleton, black hair and eyes, a swarthy complexion, short and stocky, was Jones's next listener. Hazleton's face and figure resembled his captain's, but his dress set him apart. With black beard, red kerchief about his neck and a black shirt, he was the image of a pirate in romances of the sea. Like Johnston, he maintained a bold front but found disguise a useful device. A disgruntled spectre under MacKenzie's Law, he also felt the fear that accompanies unwilling but necessary submission to an imposed order in the name of survival. Hence his piratical costume and inner capitulation. Jones presented his captain's case; Hazleton laughed. Long accustomed to seek survival by self-negation, Captain Fielding's intentions seemed to him desirable and free from serious obstacles. His spectral condition under MacKenzie or his resurrection under the commander of the *Actaeon* seemed the same to him. MacKenzie's abuse and Captain Fielding's promise of reward only differed for Hazleton in that the latter was the apparently more comfortable alternative: join or be killed by the others. Hazleton, without hesitation, signed on the *Actaeon* to be. He was blissfully free of doubt, only fearful for his life, perhaps, and so he sought security in defying his own spectre.

Jones talked with Anderson in another part of the ship. They met one night aft of the head, near the *Saladin*'s bowsprit. The Swede was the man MacKenzie had struck from the helm before the ship had reached the Horn. Like the other two men Jones had tried and found true, Anderson's colouring and hair belied his northern birth; he was dark, his eyes brown and fiery. In the darkness the two men appeared as shadows without substance excepting in the words they exchanged. Jones's brief emphasised again that refusal meant sudden death. Anderson seemed indifferent to the sail-maker's threat. Johnston's greed and Hazleton's indifference found no echo in the Swede's response to the case he hardly seemed to listen to. His apparent calmness vanished, however, when Jones referred to the quality of MacKenzie's authority. His listener's eyes burned with hatred. Apparently caring little for the promised treasure, his whole being seemed concentrated in the desire for revenge. He saw his life, body, and spirit, in the destruction of the *Saladin*'s captain, whose death would restore the Swede to the life he longed for. Anderson was the most spectral of the *Saladin*'s complement. Jones had little need to threaten the Swede, as he had the others, with death. Anderson responded to the sail-maker's question unequivocally: "By God, I'll take a knife and cut his throat. He shall no more strike me away from the helm!"

By this means Captain Fielding had arraigned and tried the skeleton crew of the as yet spectral *Actaeon*. The four men had, in their diverse ways, agreed to take part in manning their new ship. The fear of death had underlain the forms of survival they decided to live by; despising and fearing their spectral state, they chose through flesh and blood action to affirm their innocence before MacKenzie's Law that had apparently condemned them. Jones, his captain's bailiff, brought

His well-thumbed *Bible* was his constant companion, and he looked forward to the time when he could leave the sea behind forever in the same way he looked forward to salvation. This was his last voyage. Under MacKenzie's Law he shared his shipmate's spectre-making submissiveness, but his function as cook served to remind the ship's complement of the flesh and blood upon and by which their spectres survived at all. The spectacle of ghosts downing beans and salt pork presents a startling insight to the casual observer. A devoutly religious cook, as Carr certainly was, revealed the state of mind subsisting in the *Saladin*; the cook was the priest of survival, his altar a blackened stove, his missal hardtack, his sermon the food he served three times a day. And his God, his creator, was the flesh-bound authority of life itself whose command he obeyed even as the food he served kept that very flesh alive to survive another day, another storm, another voyage, another life. And MacKenzie was his prophet, the voice which spoke the gospel of transubstantiation as if directly inspired, of the gastric juice of digestion which transforms food into strength and, so to speak, life. Carr's acolyte was Galloway the steward; the cook was assisted at his mysteries by James Allen. But on the 10th of April this priest fell ill, a case, perhaps, of food poisoning. At any rate his tasks passed on to Johnston, the red-haired man whose choice of captains differed from Carr's while his reason for choosing didn't in the least. Carr knew nothing of Captain Fielding's case, the arraignment and trial of his four servants, or the plan to execute their chosen sentence, transforming the *Saladin* into the *Actaeon*.

Carr's illness conveniently permitted Johnston's constant presence in the galley as substitute cook to go virtually unnoticed. It provided a meeting place for the *Actaeon*'s men and their captain, and, on the night of Friday, the 12th, they met there as Johnston was banking his fires for the night, a half hour before his watch, the mid-watch, was to relieve the helm.

In what had become known as Carr's chapel, Captain Fielding mustered his crew. The month that had passed since he and Jones had begun the slow reconstruction of the *Actaeon* had permitted these votaries of survival to become known, one to the other. Through their common choice, they had, at least, come to tolerate if not trust one another; survival, it seems, is a somewhat personal matter. Each man looked upon the necessary sharing of rewards as condemned men look upon sharing the death sentence their crimes had previously called for. But their choice of survival under Captain Fielding still lacked the action that its creation required. They were as yet *Saladin*'s spectres; their common choice gave them a sense of vitality and deprived them of its treasure, like men whose trial was over but upon whom the verdict was as yet unspoken. Their choice created the circumstance, and now the circumstance made bodily action an urgent necessity. Their captain was this urgency, and Fielding voiced it: "This night we must act. Our common judgment has condemned the other watch, the captain and his mates. We all agreed that the freedom we seek in order to live can only come through taking this ship. As Jones told you, the other watch will act if we do not. When you go on watch at midnight we shall give Sandy the life he seeks first, then Byerby and the Carpenter. This can be done from the quarterdeck that I shall occupy. The other watch will follow their chosen master in the life he dictated for them. The ship, after all, is ours." There was no spoken response to the captain's words from the innocent executioners of MacKenzie's Law; tacit submission was enough, apparently.

it. Jones's fear was like his wooden leg: it was a hand-made device that allowed him to walk but restricted his movement. He stumped away toward the sail locker, promising to meet with the others in the galley before the mid-watch was relieved at midnight, as Captain Fielding had ordered.

Jones went aft to rouse Byerby for the watch, and then forward to feign calling the watch that already stood in their waking dream forward of the galley. Their captain used the long boat for a screen while Hazleton climbed to the poop deck to relieve Allen at the helm, followed by Johnston and Anderson. As each man passed him, Captain Fielding handed him an axe and a maul from among the Carpenter's tools under the long boat, repairs to which had been completed. Darkness helped to conceal the tools from Byerby; laying them aside out of range of the binnacle light was quickly done. Captain Fielding mounted to the poop deck using the larboard ladder, and by this means, appeared before Byerby on the quarterdeck as if he had come from the cabin. The watch was relieved quietly, Collins, Allen, and Moffat vanishing into the darkness forward; the Carpenter disappeared down the starboard steerage hatch to his bunk below the captain's cabin. All was well, and the *Saladin* and her captain and crew were ready to bring about the *Actaeon*'s resurrection. It was at this time that Captain Fielding became aware of Jones's absence. Without Jones, his agent, the remaining men could not act in safety. Neither could Captain Fielding send a man for Jones because he feared raising Byerby's curiosity.

Divided from his aim in this way, he once again felt trapped as he had before; the exercise of his authority was once again confined. The absence of an agent rendered him powerless, it seemed. In Byerby he saw MacKenzie's Law making him a passenger, invading his ship and taking it from him. Must he be bound to MacKenzie for giving him his authority? If he were so bound, his command was only a dream. But the death of MacKenzie would cancel such a bond, would make his command living, active. Thus attempting to evade the Revenue Laws of being, he silently passed the death sentence on MacKenzie once again; Byerby embodied before his eyes the passive captain who inflicted the punishment of consciousness on one possessed by dreams. The phantom

Saladin under Byerby's control at the present hour spoke of her hidden substance as irrefutably as Byerby's shadowy form commanded Captain Fielding's obedience. Authority lay outside Fielding, apparently beyond his grasp, evading possession in the very moment it seemed to offer itself to him. His eyes caught Hazleton's black head and neck dimly illuminated by the binnacle; the customary red kerchief bound around the helmsman's neck appeared blood red, as if his throat were cut. Captain Fielding stared, seeing, for a moment, his helmsman taken from him, his ship without a guiding hand. Who had killed Hazleton? The helm shifted as the ship replied to the command of wind and sea; the helmsman's hand corrected the wilful ship, and Captain Fielding's vision was corrected too by Hazleton's mere obedience to this task. Captain Fielding and the crew of his *Actaeon* were, it seemed, ghosts who watched upon the decks of a ship that wasn't theirs, prisoners serving MacKenzie's Law on what was his ship yet, the *Saladin*.

Jones's absence had rendered his captain's plan as impotent as its commander. The night passed into dawn and daylight of Saturday, April 13th. The sail-maker failed to appear until the first dog watch. His captain waited for him forward of the galley; he demanded an accounting from his agent, and the response was a measure of the man. Fear had overcome his resolution; he had felt a rope around his neck as he went forward to feign calling an already alert watch. Could murdering his shipmates free him? How? The choice of captains he had made, the agreement to act with the others in order to survive had suddenly appeared to him, perhaps in a dream, as suicide. Incurring such guilt unmanned him. In short, he was afraid. His captain's words, while hardly a consolation, overcame Jones's former fear with a fear still greater: "There's no use making a fool of yourself; if you go back your life is no more!" It seemed to the sail-maker that the crime had already been committed, as he was committed to

They met as they had the night before. Johnston banked his fires as their captain repeated his orders. Sandy was condemned first, to be followed by his mates and the starboard watch. Their crimes were known, their deaths inevitable; he and his crew were already dead by the light of the moon which they chose as their guide for their actions. Eight bells marked the hour, and three men led by their captain mounted the starboard ladder to relieve the watch. Hazleton had awakened the first mate, and then moved forward to awaken the watch that had not slept. Johnston relieved Allen at the helm and Byerby relieved the Carpenter, who had just completed his entry in the log and signed his name. "Well, good night, Tom," he said as he turned to go, "you'll be pleased to know we cross the Line at 0345 if our dead reckoning prove true. Quiet watch, and good night." The starboard watch faded away into the darkness; the larboard watch had their ship and their axes and mauls, prepared to reconstruct a ship they had never seen, commanded by a captain they did not know, and sailing trackless waters with all the world before them.

Hazleton, returning from forward, relieved Johnston at the helm. Glancing to starboard he could barely make out his captain standing behind the mate in the darkness beyond the binnacle's circle of light. Byerby moved toward the hencoop, saying, "Jack, steer her as well as you can, I do not feel very well." As he said this, he lay down on the hencoop on his back. In a short time he seemed asleep. Captain Fielding stepped forward, the dim light catching his feet and legs as high as his knees. "Johnston!" "Sir?" the red-haired man replied, stepping toward his captain from larboard. " The mate's asleep; says he's ill–cure him!" Johnston's axehead glittered in the obscurity as he raised it above his head and struck; the sound of the severed head striking the deck precisely echoed the thump of the axe as it sunk into the pine plank of the hencoop. Anderson and Jones, at shoulders and legs, lifted Byerby's vessel and let it fall into the sea. Captain Fielding grasped the head by the hair and threw it in a long sweeping arc over the stern. Wind and the voice of the ship drowned the sounds made by the jettisoned mate. "There's one gone," said Captain Fielding. His voice had taken on a new quality; it now sounded with its former strength. But a subdued calmness appeared also, like the voice of a judge seated on his Bench; Fielding's mind recalled his standing before the invaders of his ship, the *Actaeon*, off Chincha as he shot down an attacker before being wounded and captured himself. But the memory was brief, and there were other matters that required his attention. His plan had called for MacKenzie's death first, then the mate's; the commander first, then his agents. But circumstance had offered Byerby, and the offer had been accepted.

The *Actaeon*'s commander ordered Jones to relieve the helm and sent Hazleton and Anderson below to sentence MacKenzie; they disappeared down the companionway, entered the cabin's dim lamplight, tried and opened the door to the after cabin. Through the stern windows came the faint light of the equatorial night mixing with the accused. The *Saladin*'s voice filled the space between the call and the appearance of the Carpenter's head and shoulders in the open hatchway. "What do you call me for?" Anderson passed judgment on the second mate but failed in his sentence; using the back of the axe like a hammer, he struck the head a glancing blow that ended by smashing the Carpenter's left collarbone, shoulder-blade and left upper arm. He fell forward, half on deck, half in the hatchway. Hazleton stepped to starboard and the three men managed to rid themselves of their burden, whose heavy form made a loud splash as it hit the water. of all his wishes, the man and the command lived on in him, dividing him as his axe had become, for him, the joining, uniting force of life itself. The voice of the *Saladin* soothed his mind; as he stepped slightly forward, finding himself strangely forced to move by the body that confined him; the

multaneously MacKenzie's bell sounded three times in the darkness; he used it to call his steward, but Galloway slept on. No one answered the bell, but all those who heard it stood transfixed, rigid–suddenly a spectral voice arose from the sea close aboard on the starboard quarter. "Murder, murder!" A groan and silence, the Carpenter's last word.

Johnston was first to break the spell. Followed by the other two men, he sprang to the quarterdeck, seized a corner of the skylight, and, shaking it, shouted "Man overboard; man overboard, starboard side!" His captain added his shout to his mate's, stepping into the binnacle light far enough to dimly reveal his body, its head cut off at the shoulders by the shadow. The Carpenter's warning to any who might hear him of the proceedings of the court of survival, the warning that was a call for help, the dying cry was used to arouse MacKenzie from his sleep. The genesis of Captain Fielding's creation by judgment was approaching its conclusion, his agents were at hand. His desire for command, so long his ruling dream, moved from the peace of concealment and approached incarnation as a living soul. Watching at the skylight, Fielding saw MacKenzie cross the cabin in the half-light of the lamp and start up the companionway. He motioned Anderson to the hatch, Johnston relieved Jones at the helm, and the two men, Fielding behind them now fully though dimly illuminated by the binnacle light, stepped toward the opening just as MacKenzie emerged from it and stepped on deck into shadow.

The two captains stood facing one another; the one saw his authority vested in the garments of sleep, the other saw the apparently negative force of awareness which would rob him of his command. The one captain shadowed forth the other. Darkness made the blue eyes dark; the dim light made the dark eyes see, blue. Their eyes held them both, two creations of a single force manifested in the voice of the *Saladin* as she moved through the sea. "Strike him down," the captain

Si hissed in the voice of revenge; as Anderson lunged Captain MacKenzie seized his maul. "You ruffian, I'll take your life," he snarled as he and his attacker wrestled over the maul between them. "Damn your eyes, Jones, seize his arms!" The sail-maker, getting behind the captain as he struggled toward the light, pinned his arms as Anderson wrenched the maul free, discarded it, and seized the captain by the throat. The three men locked in combat stumbled to the edge of the circle of light. The one captain, axe raised over his head, awaited the propitious moment. The other, armless, eyes starting from his head, saw the glimmering axehead. "No, Fielding, no; don't take my life!" "Damn you, I'll give it to you;" as the axe fell, dividing the judged man's head in two, brains, blood and teeth splattered the deck, and one eye fell from its bloody socket and rolled to the feet of the other. The axe divided the one as it joined the two, the light and the dark, linking hand and head by an ashen handle which fell to the fouled deck as the hand released its hold. Supported between fear and revenge, the Captain's corpse hung down its head, confessing to its crime as its other eye glittered under the binnacle at the feet of its creator and judge. The word "don't" echoed in the captain's ears, but he had crossed the Line. Erect in the light, the creator, proud as a stag, had given the other his life in return for the command he coveted; the act had transformed him, and the judgment he had pronounced previously, the sentence he had handed down, had been executed.

Fielding and MacKenzie had exchanged places. The *Actaeon* was the ship he had lost and dreamed of finding in the *Saladin*. Her captain had begrudgingly allowed him on board his ship as a passenger, one MacKenzie, a captain without a ship, whose presence cut deep into the captain's mind, tendering his stroke for survival into a death-blow. The command survived still, but the man did not, apparently. Jacob Fielding had acted on his desire for security found in authority. He lost the source of command in gaining it, and in spite

unsteady feet slipped on the eye and the gore that lay between his boot and his deck. He found himself falling heavily forward on his knees and caught MacKenzie's knees in his arms for balance, head down, a suppliant. "God damn you to Hell," he groaned, "why can't you lubberly bastards drown him?" The two supporters strained toward the taffrail with their captain, who, in his attempt to stand, was dragged over the slippery decks until his grasp loosened and he found himself on all fours. He had nearly fallen over the taffrail; a thunderous splash to starboard brought him wide-eyed with fear to his feet. Leaning over the taffrail in the light of the false dawn the last he saw of himself was the glitter of a single eye watching as he receded into the pale light.

The Captain turned forward to see his ship materialize before his eyes, sails and spars whitening in the growing light. He was her master, but he felt as he recalled feeling when he was condemned to a whitened cell at Callao for conspiring to regain command of the *Actaeon*. The *Saladin*, his ship, and the remembered cell, his cell, seemed one, as he addressed the men before him. "This ship is ours, and the command is mine." The words fell hollowly on the ears of all that heard. The whiteness of the quarterdeck was dyed red with drying blood; an eye crushed to jelly near the binnacle bore witness to the captain's triumph. The bloody axe lay between the vague footprints which still showed where the two captains had stood and had fallen; another axe was embedded still in the hencoop, while still others lay scattered over the deck. The men looked like the unburied corpses of murdered men, the condemned, not the executioners. Anderson's face and clothes were smeared with the blood of Carpenter and Captain, Johnston's wore the first mate's, and the Captain's pilot cloth had changed from blue to a dark red and black from head to toe. Blood everywhere, the blood of the sentence, the blood whose authority spoke to the men who seized it for their own. Yes, the ship was theirs and the command was the captain's.

143

Once men, they had apparently given up that condition for the elusive security of the spectral state they sought to avoid. They were men still but men who had changed eyes, or whose eyes had been changed for them by the fate. The Law that had once been MacKenzie's and that had also been Fielding's, and was now MacKenzie's again; and Fielding was its puppet, this ship, the *Saladin*, like the axe he had wielded, was his master in disguise, a disguise formed by the hand of man.

"Trevaskiss, call the watch; bear a hand!" The mate, once known as Johnston in another life, moved toward the forecastle driven by the captain's command. Fielding took the helm, newly unaware of the difference between deck hand and captain, as he ordered Hazleton forward to haul down the flying jib preparatory to intercepting the oncoming watch with Trevaskiss. Jones and Anderson collected the weapons and removed the signs of judgment from the quarterdeck. The cabin had preceded the forecastle in the order of sentencing; cabin complete, forecastle must follow. The ship still bore its captain's sentence and the executioners who could carry it out; condemned men became judges, just as forecastle and cabin were now reversed. The threat of authority lay in the living, the starboard watch, whose life made them officers in Fielding's creation, just as he, in manning the helm, made himself an ordinary seaman. The vitality of his authority he saw only in Trevaskiss and Hazleton, the two he meant to make into his mates, who, in their striding forward formed the bond between cabin and forecastle, the ashen-handled axe that had united Fielding and his office. His stroke was being repeated; the two men were his instrument.

have shown here." In his piety he readily condemned the man before him who, in his turn, had fed upon that same propensity to judge. The cook's pious morality and the captain's desire for authority seemed strangely linked. Carr was looking up at his piety standing above him; it condemned him to sub-

James Allen, the cook's assistant, responded first to his mate's call. Rubbing the sleep from his eyes, he strode quickly aft and mounted the poop deck on the larboard side. Showing no sign of surprise at Fielding's presence, before relieving the helm, he helped Jones draw a bucket of seawater to wet down the quarterdeck, now cleansed of blood. It required no sign from the captain now to move Anderson. He grasped an axe, stepped silently across the deck, and struck Allen on the back of the head. The force of the blow toppled Allen over the side and the condemned Anderson nearly followed his aim, catching himself on the taffrail as Jones seized the back of his shirt. The first of the forecastle officers was, for all intents and purposes, gone. The helmsman ordered Anderson forward to help the two who preceded him with their task. Moffat's sentence was carried out by the mates, albeit they went unrecognised as such by Moffat, who saw them as his equals, not as his masters. Hazleton struck him down, and, as he did so shouted to Anderson, who, near the bowsprit, simultaneously struck Collins who was at the head. He fell into the sea without a cry. The present threat to the helmsman was quelled, it seemed, as the *Saladin* sailed over the sinking Collins. His command was secure although his doubts had not yet been exorcised.

The appearance of Fielding's son on deck while his mates were forward had terrified him, as the ghost of a murdered man might chill the blood of his executioner; only the boy's eyes, dark like his father's, seemed alive to the helmsman. Those eyes clove his soul, bright and sharp, bringing blindness and death to the father, shutting out the daylight as if he once again had donned the poncho his son brought to help him escape from his prison at Callao; his rescuer he now perceived to be his judge. "Get below and bring us brandy," he snarled, "the ship is mine. We've had a night of it, and a bellyful of passing judgment–it's time for some spirit! Go!" The boy disappeared without a word and returned with two bottles of MacKenzie's treasured l'*eau-de-vie*. The three executioners returned to the quarterdeck in time to drink with their captain; Jones had relieved the helm. The liquor burned their throats, giving their spectral spirits the illusion of life and vitality. Brandy and the *Saladin* carried them forward, inspiring the condemned judges. "I am now commander of this ship," said Fielding," and my first mate is Trevaskiss; my second mate is Hazleton. Vengeance is mine, and infractions against my authority will be treated as were Sandy's." Anderson grimaced but remained silent. Trevaskiss reminded his captain of the deeds they had performed in his service. All were equal before the Law, were they not? The captain, scowled but said nothing. His second mate then reminded him of Carr and Galloway, the cook and steward, still sleeping forward. "Cooks and stewards are moralists without a function on this ship; I will deal with them when they show themselves. They must obey me now, as you must." As he spoke he glanced forward to see Carr hurriedly passing his chapel where he usually relighted the fires, his daily task at 0600. As the devout man reached the ladder leading to the quarterdeck, he looked up. "That's far enough." Fielding's command stopped him in his tracks, fear plainly showing in the cook's face; the fear came from the sight of Moffat's blood, not from the command to halt. The cook had seen the blood on the bulkhead and bulwarks to starboard.

"What's the blood to starboard, Captain Fielding?" asked Carr. "The last of a rebel's spirit, Carr. I am commander, now, on this ship. Sandy and his fellow-conspirators have been summarily dealt with as the guilty must ever be. We've finished them. Now you must either join us or you're a dead man–what do you say, cook?" Carr saw the captain's complement behind him, Hazleton holding a bottle and Anderson an axe. Elijah's reproof to Ahab came to the cook's mind, and so did his children waiting his return. "I want none of this work," he said, "and may God have more mercy on your soul than you

mission or to death. The cook and the captain were one in the form they chose to achieve their desire; Carr, sensing his captain's feeling, and seeing, albeit unrecognised, his piety thus standing before him, dismissed the man, the criminal, from his mind and submitted to the authority above him. As he climbed the ladder to the quarterdeck, Galloway, the steward, approached the after cabin, having emerged from his hiding place in the galley. He laughed as he joined his devout master, having heard the captain's words and seen the cook's submission: "Blessed are the pure in heart, for they shall see God, eh, Bill? And you've agreed to cook for Him! Well, I'll serve up what you cook; our good captain's digestion is only transubstantiation in disguise!" Carr scowled at his assistant's blasphemies as Captain Fielding called all hands to swear to mutual trust and loyalty, hands on the Holy Book his cook lent him for the purpose.

The oath taken, the captain still appeared somehow dissatisfied; he needed more assurance than an oath could give him. Addressing Hazleton he said, "Throw the weapons overboard, Jack; I'll fetch the ship's muskets from the after cabin– we might become envious, you know." The captain and his son disappeared down the companionway and proceeded to the after cabin where three muskets and MacKenzie's fowling piece were stowed under the liquor cabinet. The key was in the lock. Passing the three muskets to his son, the captain took the fowling piece and another bottle of brandy and laid them on MacKenzie's bunk. Sending the boy topside, he bent over the chart. The ship's position had been plotted by MacKenzie's dead reckoning until noon of Sunday, the 14th, three hours away. A glance at the tell-tale showed the *Saladin* to be on her course. The captain, alonc now, rcturned swiftly to the arms locker, withdrew two pistols from a built-in case to the left of the empty musket rack, slammed the door shut and locked it. He turned, then, to the lazarette, found the copper box containing powder and ball, loaded the two pistols, and moved into the main cabin. A glance above him showed no observer at the skylight–where did he feel command lay now? Safe from observation, he took the two pistols he saw as his source of authority and placed them beneath the table.

Another glance at the skylight for assurance, and Fielding returned to the after cabin for the brandy. As he started for the companionway, he saw Galloway blocking the ladder. He had closed the after cabin door behind him; the steward had seen nothing. Motioning the steward to follow him, the captain stepped into his stateroom. Galloway sensed the man's agitation. The captain quickly told him of the valuable cargo and of his first mate's plan to kill Galloway and the cook. "With your help, the Swede's and Jack's, we can kill the others–what do you say?" The captain's appetite apparently required a steward's services, but the Irishman refused. "And the meek shall inherit the earth, eh, Captain? I'll have none of it. We're outnumbered anyway." He turned away, apparently untouched by the survival fever that made Fielding so desperate. "I'll fetch your breakfast. Perhaps that will bring you to your senses; there's nothing like food to temper judgment, is there? Carr's cooking it now." With this the steward slammed the door behind him. The captain had dreamed of successful mutiny in this same cabin as the *Saladin* rounded Cape Horn; the gales still blew within him. Now he was again a mutineer, but he was rebelling against a forecastle that had become the cabin; the officers he wanted to destroy were in authority by his own appointment. A swallow of brandy seemed to steady him, or his purpose; former dream and present intention fused within him. The stateroom's narrow dimensions confined him too closely. He tried the door; it was jammed. A growing sense the cabin table, and a loaded fowling piece in the after cabin bunk. They had joined Fielding in the name of surviving MacKenzie's turning to curses and blows to maintain his command. What they had done was to put pistols in Fielding's hands; their desire for security created the man who claimed

of restriction gave rise to desperation and fear. Using his body as a battering ram, he burst into the cabin and stumbled against the table that broke his forward rush. Recovering his balance, he once more looked up. The skylight revealed Anderson peering down at him; a gesture brought the Swede before him. The mutinous captain, as he had unsuccessfully before with the steward, voiced his plan to Anderson; he failed to recognise the man's hatred of vested authority. "If we kill all but Jones and my son, the money's ours. We'll be safe, even free. Can I count on you for our mutual well being? Trevaskiss can't be trusted, and Hazleton is with him." The Captain's reliance on his dream of mutiny inflamed by MacKenzie's brandy turned his listener into what Fielding saw as a willing servant, ready to exercise his axe again in the service of the Law of security.

Anderson's voice came to him out of a cloud of sunlight: " Not on your life–you speak like Sandy, who killed us all with his bloody Law. Your axes and muskets are all over the side anyway–it was you who feared envy! You'll not get my hand in your damned service." The Swede turned to go, but the cook's arrival with Fielding's breakfast prevented his departure. He left only when his captain sat down to eat, served by Carr. "Where's Galloway?" The cook had told the steward to clean away Moffat's persistent blood, a warning of a voice that had gone unheard. As Fielding ate, Carr went forward to fetch coffee. Returning to the cabin from the galley, he saw the captain go into the after cabin. He spent some time behind the closed door, then reappeared to greet the cook and drink the coffee, saying "Doing a bit of dead reckoning, Carr; we're heading for the Gulf of St. Lawrence. Another month and a half will bring us to safe harbour, eh? And now for the money." The two men dragged the sealed bags of mail and the sealed boxes of currency from the after cabin. Fielding looked through the letters for cash that many of them contained, money sent home by distant sons and fathers; the money they contained the captain stowed in MacKenzie's footlocker with the cook's help. The letters he burned. Breaking the seals on the boxes of currency, he placed their contents in the footlocker as well. "Two thousand pounds! A sum of weight and moment, eh?" the captain asked. His cook agreed. Three bells sounded as Fielding, followed by Carr, mounted to the quarterdeck. His plan was only held in abeyance; he felt that circumstance would give rise to the hand he sought, and fear would do the rest. The money was, after all, what those scoundrels wanted. With this in mind he ordered Trevaskiss below, instructing him to count the money for himself. Carr relieved Jones at the helm, Anderson went forward to help Galloway scrub down the galley. Hazleton and Fielding's son stood by to execute their captain's orders to shift sail. The first mate's distrust of his captain would sink before the sight of the money in the cabin. So the mutinous captain thought as he took the sun's altitude to determine his position; but his position was founded on the power of money, the creator of ease and security; his authority was now a medium of exchange.

Three hours later the captain and all his men except Carr, at the helm, and Galloway, in the galley, were seated at the cabin table. The afternoon sun shone into the space through the skylight tinting the table top, the men's glasses, their faces and eyes with gold. The money had been counted and the shares determined; the captain was telling his crew their position and informing them of his choice of destination, as he had Carr earlier. Drink made them talkative and as they quarrelled as to whether the St. Lawrence or Cape Breton was the better choice, the first mate rose and motioned to Hazleton who followed him topside. Fielding nodded his approval; winds shift and vary toward sundown; his mates would see to the furling of topgallants anticipating nightfall. But Trevaskiss had more on his mind than seamanship. Out of Carr's hearing, he told of discovering two loaded pistols hidden under

to command them, and he maintained that power by means of pistol and ball, albeit secretly. The first mate's discovery and the second mate's knowing of it now showed them Fielding in what was apparently his true light. The two mate's instinct for survival arose; they agreed to face Fielding with their knowledge, deadly, perhaps, as his pistols could ever be. Armed with their purpose, they descended the companionway.

Fielding rose as they reached the cabin; the first mate moved to the after cabin as Hazleton raised the pistols from their hiding place. "These pistols mean something," he snarled, staring at Fielding. The captain stepped back a pace. "I know nothing of these pistols; throw them overboard after the muskets and have done." The second mate pointed the weapons threateningly, the sun glinting on the bluish barrels– MacKenzie's darkened eyes flashed before Fielding's mind as the two had faced one another on the quarterdeck–Fielding blanched, but stood his ground. "Throw me overboard, why don't you? I'd rather drown than serve under you, a prisoner." The accusing pistols Fielding's mutinous command transformed into a deadly threat, and showed forth the man he had been and his rebellion against that man he had planned in the name of authority, of money. He stood now, proud and defiant as a stag that has turned at bay before the dogs thirsting for his blood, his life. But he was judged, and the witnesses against him now face him, purposes and pistols, one and the same. The first mate offered MacKenzie's loaded fowling piece in evidence; Anderson told of Fielding's mutinous intentions he had refused to agree to earlier. Trevaskiss, alias Johnston, was his judge; mutiny had transmogrified into an assertion of the authority embodied in life itself, a force that brooks no commander, whether in cabin or forecastle.

Fielding had gone from dream to axe to mate to money as he had gone from Chincha to Pisco to Callao to Valparaiso.

The creation that had brought him a sense of life in the circumstance around him turned him into a creature whose creator faced him, condemning him in the name of the life he desired and sought in the command he lost. Authority is slavery, it seemed. Fielding felt bound hand and foot; his first mate and his second seized him, threw him to the deck, and tied his hands and feet. The command of the *Saladin* lay like a ghost, nameless, visible as spectres are and as elusive, between Fielding and Trevaskiss. The former protested loudly, screaming that they would all die without a captain who knew the sea; a gag smothered his voice, as it did his helpless son's, bound beside him. The father and the son were one; resurrected from the grave of a life in command alone, the father saw not the threatening ghost he had seen on the quarterdeck. But the life to which he had given form before his eyes, his in his son's separation from him; the threat was in the father's desire to possess that life–but mutiny was the life of authority; they could never be one, apparently. Fielding and his son ceased their struggles, while the first mate of the *Saladin*, Trevaskiss alias Johnston, organised his men into watches. The disposition of Fielding and his son could be determined in the light of further thought; a mutineer can never be too circumspect. Meanwhile the father and son, passengers again, were stowed in their stateroom. The pistols, fowling piece, powder and ball followed the muskets.

The first mate shared the authority as he shared the money and the clothing the men found which had been scattered about the after cabin when Fielding had turned MacKenzie's footlocker into a money box. Brandy changed to rum; Galloway went topside to take the unmanned helm. A dead calm had confined the *Saladin* with loosely hanging sails, stowing them in the forward hold and putting them ashore at the first chance. But Carr's view was different: his pious submission to Fielding, and the erstwhile captain's counter-mutiny earned the hatred that guilt and self-deception bear. "I

dead in the water, motionless; it was during this three-hour period that Captain Fielding became the cargo his second mate made him. He was as passive as the ship to which he had given his life. Now light airs and darkness set the blocks slapping against spars and masts, sail flapping, and running rigging groaning as the *Saladin* came to life once more. The steward, less drunk than his companions, had heard the ship and obeyed her command, hand on helm.

In the cabin below his shipmates slept, surfeited with rum, brandy and the food Carr had prepared for them. No sound was heard from the father and son, but only Trevaskiss could have heard them if they had called out. He, alone, stood over the chart table under the dim light of a tiny overhead lamp squinting at the dead reckoning projection of the *Saladin*'s course begun by MacKenzie and extended by Fielding. Now that the first mate and his comrades had possession of the ship and their freedom, where should they head? London, their original destination, was clearly outlawed; the lion's mouth, the king of beasts, was no longer a refuge. The Caribbean was patrolled by the Royal Navy. Trevaskiss found himself forced to accede to Fielding's plan; the Gulf of St. Lawrence must do. Painting the figurehead of the *Saladin* they had all followed from Valparaiso, and covering the ship's name painted under the stern windows would provide safety at sea. Trevaskiss was struck by the force of the necessity for disguise, for concealment. If he and his comrades were to reach safety or were to survive at all, they must obey. First, they must obey the need for disguise, and, second, they must be under a more specific authority, a captain.

Trevaskiss's long sea-going experience had taken him from desertion at Valparaiso to deck hand, first mate and now, he saw, captain, the successor to MacKenzie. Byerby's death made him first mate, he had seen to that; MacKenzie's death had confirmed his new authority. Fielding's pistols were at his head, and he, Trevaskiss, would succeed his passenger.

Thus he embodied three men; the fourth watched over the three, conscious of the concealment, the disguise that the three manifested. His desertion from the *U.S.S. Constellation* in the name of getting home to England, his adopting an alias, was the first. The others followed. The sight of Byerby's head falling in a long arc over the stern came to him; he had denied his own eyes, and now, he saw, his life was founded on denial of name, of man, of himself. Yes, the *Saladin* must be masked if she and her inmates were to reach safety; and Trevaskiss was her commander. He drank again from the bottle set beside the chart on the polished top of the chart table. As he started to replace it, he saw his reflection in the surface of the table; his face and eyes were dark beneath matted blood-stained hair. The wet circle the bottle left on the tabletop appeared like a halter around his neck; the image of security. The bottle replaced and the image masked, he glanced again at the ship's position, his position, on the chart. The *Saladin*, at 0300 on Monday, April 15th, was one hundred miles north of the Line, seeking, above all, safe harbour.

Opening the door, Trevaskiss re-entered the cabin. Clothes, bottles, and men lay everywhere; scraps of partly burned envelopes left from Fielding's burning of the mails were scattered like dried sea-salt on the decks after a storm. Here was chaos, indeed, demanding order; the dim lone light revealed a hand here, a forehead there, and the faint shapeless shapes of the sleeping men. Through the skylight the stars peered down, pale pinpoints of light fading in the glow of the rising moon. The telltale witnessed Galloway's competence at the helm. The first mate roused Anderson, Hazleton and Jones quickly; Carr was slower to awake. The four men rose to their feet, looked about, and once again sat at the table as Trevaskiss turned up the lamp; he then took the captain's chair. A unanimous vote made him their chief; the rank of captain was not mentioned. Once this was completed, the problem of disposing of Fielding and his son was raised. Jones suggested

won't rest easy until they are thrown overboard. The father's the devil incarnate," he said, " and as long as he's on this ship not one of us is safe." Silence followed the cook's plea, then agreement. The Law once again prevailed. Their chief and his second, Hazleton, saw an opportunity to establish their ascendancy over the only men on the *Saladin* who, as yet, had not joined the others as executioners. Unity in guilt is, apparently, a binding force among spectres whose lives arise from death, a guilt that is their only sign of life.

Hazleton awakened the father and son, loosening the bonds at their feet enough to permit walking, however awkwardly; Jones led the father and Hazleton the son to the quarterdeck. Galloway stood at the helm, guiding the ship under the bright moonlight. Anderson took a post to larboard as Jones moved the father to the taffrail. Trevaskiss stood facing Fielding, standing between his helmsman and the captain, who now faced forward. The moonlight turned all faces pale and all eyes dark. As Carr emerged from the companionway, his chief ordered him to help Jones with Fielding; the cook seized his left arm; Hazleton and the son watched the scene from forward of the hencoop; Trevaskiss now ordered Galloway to take Jones's place in carrying out the sentence, but Galloway refused. "I'll have no part in your necessities, Bill; I'm a steward, not a mate." "We'll see," said the chief, "who's who aboard this ship!" He turned and fixed Fielding with his eyes; the captain of the *Actaeon* returned a defiant stare, at bay before his own dogs, saying, "You're a dead man, Johnston, and you know it–you can only give me my life, not take it–and so lose your own. But the self-condemned, like the self-appointed captain, has neither eyes to see nor ears to hear. If you must do this, at least save my son." "Enough," cried Johnston, "it's over with you!" The two men faced one another as Fielding had faced MacKenzie. The captain of the *Actaeon* felt a pervading sense of life as he recognised the servant that made him. He was the servant who is the master;

155

being lifted over the taffrail, he felt himself falling backward, down, until the waters closed over his head. He rose slowly to the surface and saw the *Saladin*, a ghost ship in the brilliant moonlight, slowly diminish as he receded from it into the light. Fielding and MacKenzie were one in life as in command.

As Fielding disappeared over the stern, Hazleton stepped aft to see the end. The son, left untended, moved forward as quickly as he could, hobbled as he was. At first he escaped notice; but Galloway saw his head disappear down the starboard ladder and gave the alarm; Carr ran forward after the boy; Anderson took the helm Galloway had deserted in following Carr. They caught Fielding beside the starboard forechains. He screamed and attempted to resist the two men, but to no avail. "You fiends," he shouted, "my father's hand be on you," and he was gone. Carr and Galloway returned to the poop deck slowly, fully initiated members of the *Saladin*'s crew, the judges and executioners whose sentences were axes and strong arms, whose trials were mutinies, and whose Law was possession. They met their chief justice at the binnacle, and the *Saladin* had what seemed to be, standing there in the light of the moon beside his helmsmen, a new commander, Captain Trevaskiss. Under his authority they sought, as he did, Harbour Island, unaware.

every self-possessed moralist, I sought to make good my escape. For me, the *Saladin* seemed to offer, at first, the means ness notwithstanding. Being the observer, as every writer must be, gives me distance and safety that somehow has been otherwise denied me. Even the warmth of this August evening chills me; its clear light befogs my mind's eye–am I dying, or

CHAPTER FOUR

The Meeting

It is said that a wicked man who was unfortunately a passenger, seduced you from your obedience to the captain with whom you sailed–to the God who created you, and plunged you into crimes of barbarity and atrocity from the contemplation of which the mind recoils.

The Sentence

The Golden Inn, Lunenburg, 9 August, 1844: Tonight I take up my pen here at home to bring to a halt, if not a conclusion, my struggle with the case of the *Saladin* and myself. I had seen the newspaper reports, and recalled the circumstances that made for double mutiny on board the *Saladin*. Mutiny called me to make that long journey to Halifax and to return as well from a scene of imprisonment, trial, and death to write of them here. And so to see them before me, perhaps even to place them beyond judgment where they belong.

My search among the moral wreckage which form is still embodied in the sometime survivors of the *Saladin* has not brought to light much that is salvageable. Is it fear that makes men into murderers? I ask myself this question still, after piercing the fog, braving heavy seas, and finally boarding the *Saladin*'s case to see what tale and what treasure she contained. I meet once again as I met there the dispossessed, the lust for gold, for possession, an Eden of no return. Like

to re-establish the security her actions apparently mocked.

Trials, like newspapers, give facts, but my dilemma is of another order; how far apart do I stand from the survivors or, for that matter, their victims? "For where your treasure is, there will your heart be also." I once thought I commanded an unquestionable and authoritative understanding of that sentence; the survivors, the men of law as well as myself, belie that authority. Wasn't ours a common search for treasure and theirs the desire for security and life while mine was for the coin of righteousness? Seeking safe harbour for myself, I find I have run ashore under full sail. No longer in command but now under the authority of my desperate need for rectitude, carried to a hostile shore and forced over on my beam ends by a sense of order. Doesn't the suspicion of sharing a common goal, the judges and I, require at least another look at the Bill of Lading as it must contrast with present cargo? So it would seem to me, since the desire to survive is, perhaps, generally accepted as legitimately human. But the Law supports, nay even is my contention, and I have seen four men hanged to ensure its existence. If the survivors and I share a goal why don't we share the end such a goal forms? Am I, like them, a victim of circumstance? And if so, what are those bonds, self-made as they seem to be? Is this security, I desperately ask myself?

It appears to me now that I met a stranger in the *Saladin*, a stranger whose acquaintance I didn't want, God knows, and whose presence makes claims of authority I resist as I would resist a threat to my life. He insinuates that my rectitude is borne up by his death under law; where, then, does authority lie? It seems that if I rebel against his contention I make an end of myself in any reasonably acceptable form.

As I have come to see, the *Saladin* has made and still makes an apparently inescapable prison for me. Telling of it is a trial and condemnation in itself; and perhaps the tale will resolve what reason cannot, Courts, Sentences, and righteous-

struggling for security in a world I did not make? Where is He who made me? Has He seen fit to leave me in this prison? Or will imagination once again allow me respite, a reprieve from the sentence which security hands down and desire executes? Will this reprieve come from my being enabled to see myself, to meet myself, perhaps, beyond security but once more a living man? Let me see.

Valparaiso, 7 February, 1844: On the Strada Valdivia near the dockyards is found an obscure public house much frequented by sea-going men. "The Sign of the Trap" was, at one time, a small Customs House and its present owner hasn't seen fit to modify the interior. Opening a central street door, a seeker for reprieve finds himself in what the dim light reveals as a narrow space bounded on left and right by oaken tables with benches behind them running from the front wall to a long, transverse counter at the rear of the room. Once used for the inspection and evaluation of goods for revenue entering or leaving port, the tables now provide a polished surface circled by the liquor glasses of customers whose circles are their only monument. Behind the counter a dais supports a throne-like seat where His Honour the Proprietor sits, surveying customers and the servant who waits on them. The resemblance between his public house and a court of law is not apparent to a casual pleasure-seeker. But it is clear to almost any regular visitor who finds in dimness light and in drink the creation of a world closer to the heart's desire–furthermore a world where his judgment goes unquestioned. Beginning in a formless void of every day dry docks, the survivor arises fully sea-worthy to face whatever his eyes may show him; and so he returns to the world outside under full sail only to run ashore, his cargo falling into other hands. Once again he is dispossessed and on trial for piracy and murder.

Captain Isaac MacKenzie, commanding officer of the barque *Saladin*, had been drinking most of that Thursday afternoon. A native of Nairn, he epitomised the rigidity of demeanour that only Scottish Presbyterian rectitude (he was a near relative of the Rev. John MacKenzie of Free Church, Dumfries) together with the god-like authority of command at sea could create. His character, unshaken by twenty years at sea, had been hardened by experience and the security born of proven competence into the self-possession that survival sometimes creates. His blue eyes were his most striking feature. Deeply set, they arrested an observer's attention and rendered his ruddy face, grizzled beard and unexpectedly slender build almost like signs of an acquittal in the face of an expected death sentence. Drinking mitigated this sentence, reconciling within him judge and condemned.

The summer afternoon had become evening when a stranger entered "The Sign of the Trap" which up to that time had been nearly deserted. MacKenzie sat near the counter on the starboard bench, aft, and alone in the obscurity, as if his long life at sea had trained him to find a quarterdeck wherever he found himself. "Mind?" MacKenzie looked up at the intrusive voice facing him across the table. Through the gloom he saw a stout, well-built man, with prominent, and rather strongly marked, but by no means unpleasant features. The expression of the face indicated great decision of character given witness by a pair of bright, black eyes and thick, bushy dark eyebrows dominating a swarthy, weather-beaten complexion. "Sit down!" The recognition was more command than acceptance; the unyielding juncture of the prosecutor and the accused.

Provided with drink of his own, the stranger broke the possession of the former the creation of the latter—and what sort of government was that? Prison, yes, but escape, or resolution? His son was the resolution, and perhaps the command, the authority of but not in him. He came to see that the poncho and the shavings that hid him from government authority perhaps had begun to show a controlling power of their own. Could it be that he was simply the creature of his circum-

pervading, silent void between the two men. Deferentially, he inquired of MacKenzie's ship, recognising by costume and air his companion's way of life. The captain told of the barque *Saladin*, 550 tons burthen, out of Newcastle-on-Tyne and making her return voyage to London, sailing on Friday evening, with a cargo of copper, guano and specie, manned by two mates and nine souls, two of whom had joined the ship at Valparaiso. After twenty years at sea, the speaker was making his final voyage and proposed settling down with his family in Newcastle. His listener showed an awakened interest as MacKenzie's account proceeded. His eyes brightened; he moved forward in his chair apparently stirred by the speaker's words. MacKenzie, observing this response, continued with an account of his preacher father, his choosing the sea as a way of life and his rise to command at the age of thirty through the drowning of his captain in a gale off the Cape of Good Hope in '29. Although a disaster had made him a captain, he chose to see his new-found authority as a well-deserved gift of God, the rightness of which he had never questioned: the man had become the Captain, created so by divine sanction and a gale at sea. His present crew he condemned as scoundrels controlled only by his moral ascendancy over them; swift punishment for any infraction ensured ready if unwilling obedience to the voice of command.

Such unquestioning certitude called forth signs of tacit deference in his listener. More drink appeared as he sat back, surveyed MacKenzie from beneath lowering brows that concealed the mockery in his eyes. He nevertheless deferred to the speaker's assertions, submitting to these winds of nautical dogma as a skilful captain must bend his will and his ship to the only force which can give him what he seeks. He seemed both to judge and support MacKenzie's Law.

His support imaged forth MacKenzie's self-portrait; they could have been one man. He, too, had commanded a barque, the *Actaeon*, out of Liverpool, carrying a crew of sixteen and his fifteen-year-old son. To him as to MacKenzie, the power of life and death over his crew seemed the only means to gain the dual advantages of authority and money. Having sought freight in Buenos Aires and Valparaiso in vain, the *Actaeon* had proceeded to Chincha, off the coast of Peru, in search of guano, the excrement of tropical sea birds valuable in the manufacture of fertiliser and gunpowder, two means men have found to promote the cause of survival. An infraction of the Revenue Laws of Peru led to a gunshot wound received when he attempted to save his command from Peruvian government forces. The wound was looked after in a convent at Pisco. Later he was taken in the *Actaeon* to Callao, where the speaker's single-minded desire to regain his command led him into conspiracy, discovery and imprisonment. His son and a poncho allowed his escape, while carpenter's shavings in the dockyard concealed him, until he found return passage in a British ship to Valparaiso. A captain without a command, a fugitive whose means to salvation had been his son, a fifteen-year-old boy. His being constantly possessed by the desire for command had brought him to his present condition. He had transformed circumstance into a means to an end by reducing events, like the sea, to serving him and his aims. He regarded men as he did circumstance, apparently, both being servants of an overmastering desire to possess golden authority.

Chincha was the island where his authority ran afoul of a governing force he chose to overlook, ignoring, or at least attempting to ignore, the confinement that the ideal of authority gained through infraction creates. Callao, therefore, found him in a conspiratorial prison from which only the son could rescue his father. Buried beneath the scraps tossed aside in a construction that had failed to be sea-worthy, the by-product of his aim, like his son, had preserved him. His imprisonment was the sentence of a court the laws of which he had served, uniquely enough, as both judge and accused. It appeared to him that authority based on infraction made the

stance and not the creator using them but a creature used by them? But he had made his escape, regardless; his trial was apparently over; the prison sentence mitigated by the ingenuity of blood, the skilfully conceived arguments of generation which had won the case, silencing the mortal brief of prosecution based on the absolute link between authority and infraction. He made good his escape by finding passage to Valparaiso for himself and his son in the *Diana*, a British schooner carrying guano bound for Dublin.

In Valparaiso he had passed the last four days seeking a return passage to Liverpool. His search had been a further trial for him, forcing him to take the deferential stance foreign to a commander. Haunting the docks, he had approached a Captain Ward of the hermaphrodite brig *Jeremiah Garnett* who had refused him. No outlaw would find refuge in Ward's command. A Captain Troy of the *Sinon* took aversion to his mocking deference and pride. Void of hope, the stranger had fallen by chance on "The Sign of the Trap" which he hadn't observed before. He now sought a ship and passage from his listener. "Will you make a father and his son passengers?"

MacKenzie responded to the stranger's narrative in unmoving silence. The blue eyes seemed to deny the request for passage. In his companion he saw a renegade, but a renegade in whose crime he could not avoid perceiving the stubborn refusal to recognise any obstacle to attaining command. To him command was life, the gift of a Creator who had first granted dominion over creation to the sun and moon and then to Adam and Eve. Such authority, therefore, was of divine origin, and the unremitting demand for it as a possession had, in itself, a certain force for MacKenzie. The circle from his glass on the polished oak enclosed the image of eyes in a ghostly face; his glass, filled and replaced again, showed the eyes floating beneath the still turbulent and bubbling surface of his liquor, their blue turned to darkness. The servant awaited payment; the stranger paid and drank. MacKenzie disliked his disdainfully deferential partner in spite of the love of authority he sensed in the man's tale. The infraction against Revenue Laws stamped him as immoral, a sinner and an outlaw. His desperate defence of the *Actaeon* at Chincha, his conspiring to recapture his ship at Callao, and the escape from deserved confinement all pointed to ingrained rebelliousness. But rebellion against whom and for what purpose? Wasn't the desire for a command as much the equivalent of self-preservation for his companion opposite him as it was for MacKenzie himself? And self-preservation is sanctioned by Law; the ship is forever its commander's charge. His opposite's action showed his allegiance to this Law of the sea, and, therefore, he seemed a man worthy of respect; but what then of his crimes? Didn't they still exist?

The captain of the *Saladin* wrestled silently in the formlessness of irresolution. His command of the issues because of the man before him became tenuous to him, even equivocal. Just as the question condemned his assertion of command over it, so his command necessarily relegated the question to inconsequence. His life in the possession of authority acquired through twenty years at sea and the accidental drowning of his captain by which he had been possessed of it determined his resolution. The desire for the security of authority, a central and commanding ideal, became a moral principle of life for Captain MacKenzie.

The February summer night, cloudy and darkly starless, had long closed in upon the two captains. His Honour the Proprietor had seen to additional lamps in his establishment, making it less obscure as the blackness outside intensified. The room was now nearly full of shapeless drinkers seeking to usurp the everyday world. Light and sound engulfed MacKenzie and his companion. The Captain of the *Saladin* looked across the mirroring table-top at the other man, who repeated his former question: "Will you make a father and his son passengers?" "Welcome on board the *Saladin*, Captain! But now you must give me your name; Isaac MacKenzie, at your service." "Fielding," was all he said.

FINIS

Afterword

Congratulations, reader! You have just completed a formidable and arduous voyage of the imagination, tracing backwards through time, space and the savage necessities of maritime law, recreating the portentous last cruise of the British barque *Saladin* in 1844. You have relived the experience of rounding the Horn under sail, pounded by merciless seas driven by ice-laced winds, then entering the deceptive ease of working northwards in the relative calm of the South Atlantic, crossing the Line after witnessing not one but two brutal mutinies, each accompanied by treachery and murder. You have relived the experience of losing your way, intellectually, morally, physically, beating in intoxication across "the trackless deep, with all the world before you," until you come smashing ashore on the rocky verge of the ironically-named Harbour Island. You have relived the experience of boarding the grounded *Saladin*, apprehending the drunken mutineers, attending their trial in Halifax, and following the condemned to the garrison city's last public hanging. And you have done all this by living vicariously through the journal of Solomon Scharf, "a man from Lunenburg, who teaches and sometimes talks, sometimes writes."

And how that man does write. The twistings and turnings of this complex tale are aptly mirrored in the twistings and turnings of Scharf's prose, once he doggedly settles down to the task of wringing meaning out of multifaceted tragedy as profoundly challenging as the trackless deep itself. A poetic visionary, intent upon pursuing his own insights wherever and however they might lead, this Lunenburg schoolmaster thinks largely in terms of simile and metaphor: when he sees something, he also instantly sees it as something else – a kaleidoscope of perception, object clicking into object, one individual blending into another, patterns forming and reforming, incessantly reminding us of the indivisible unity of all things. Commencing with his own vivid reconstruction of the imprisoned mutineers vying among themselves to confess, a reconstruction based on his readings of the local newspapers, he becomes the reader's reader, hearing each confession, seeing each accused bear witness against himself and others, noting the mounting gratification of the authorities with the apparent ease of trying such a case. But the gratification of High Sheriff, Attorney-General and Lloyd's Official Agent, gathering together the written acknowledgments of guilt so freely offered, only serves as sharp contrast to the mortified perplexity of our Solomon, now gradually becoming alert to the dismaying prospect of gallows fruit as food for thought. Named for wisdom and acuity, he takes us deep into dark convolutions of our own justice system, bringing to light matters that we might not otherwise have noticed.

The grim facts, to be sure, seem straightforward enough. The *Saladin*, commanded by Captain Isaac MacKenzie, sailed from Chile for England with two other officers and a crew of nine. She carried a cargo of guano fertiliser, a partial ballast of copper ingots, and an impressive treasure in silver bars and gold Mexican dollars: moreover, she also carried two passengers, another Captain named Jacob Fielding and his fifteen year old son. Jealous of MacKenzie's command and determined to possess the treasure, Fielding threatened and persuaded one watch of the crew to mutiny, killing MacKenzie, his two mates and three loyal sailors of the other watch, callously tossing the bodies overboard. Determined to reduce still farther the numbers sharing the loot, Fielding tried to entice some of the mutineers to turn against their comrades, which merely convinced his accomplices to band together and rid themselves of this new menace: hence, Fielding and his son quickly followed the other victims overboard. But that left the *Saladin* without anyone who could navigate, resulting in the barque crashing ashore at the entrance of Country Harbour, Nova Scotia. To the authorities apprehending the survivors, maritime law need only proceed with the same rigorous dispatch as that dictated by the inflexible logic of the murderous crewmen themselves. In the words of the Swedish mutineer Anderson, "There were fourteen persons on board the *Saladin* when we left Valparaiso; six of them are here – eight of them are not here: they were killed." How much more straightforward could it all be? "Just a matter of mathematics," marvels Solomon Scharf: "fourteen minus eight leaves six."

Mathematics of that sort could make equal disposition of all the *Saladin's* survivors as well, under the dictates of maritime law. Mutiny, piracy and murder were punishable by death, and all six survivors were confessed mutineers, pirates and murderers: hence, six minus six leaves nothing, a logic that judge and Attorney-General would strive to apply. But Solomon Scharf, who had initially come to a similar conclusion after reading of the case, cannot remain content with this stark simplicity. Attending the trial of the six, he follows with painstaking metaphoric logic the gymnastics of the law, which affords his incisive imagination ample scope for intriguing gyrations of his own. Two of the survivors, Carr and Galloway, cook and steward respectively, had taken no part in the first mutiny: below decks when the opening massacre occurred, they immediately surrendered to Fielding and the other mutineers, pledging allegiance to the enterprise. When Fielding's further machinations became known, the original mutineers forced Carr and Galloway to throw Fielding and his son overboard, seeking to implicate them through murder in everything that had been done. Courtesy of those developments, Carr and Galloway sought to plead innocence, arguing they had only acted in self-defence to ensure their own survival. This was a plea our Solomon would pursue relentlessly, since it rests upon a principle everyone accepts intuitively: "we all spend our lives in pious worship of security and obedience to its Law."

While recognizing the plausibility of what cook and steward were claiming, Scharf is quick to understand that the argument has extremely disconcerting ramifications. In the crude reasoning of Carr and Galloway, they were innocent of any crime: they acquiesced in mutiny and piracy, yes; and worse still, they killed a man and a boy, yes; but these acts could not be deemed criminal, since they were committed to save the perpetrators' own lives, and from no other motive. And yet, the other mutineers, listening to the presentations of their purportedly unwilling accomplices, waste no time entering similar pleas in extenuation of their own crimes. It was Fielding who threatened them with death if they didn't comply with his plans, they insisted. "He told them the other watch was ready if they refused, the other watch, standing in the dock; the other watch standing by to take over control of the ship if safety became danger." Hence, the original victims were cast in the role of potential menace, later to be slaughtered by the mutineers "drawn into crime by the force of circumstance." Hearing this analysis offered with all due solemnity by counsel for the defense at the Admiralty Court in Halifax, Scharf is moved to exclaim inwardly: "Not men but circumstances are the creators of action, of life!" These are intellectual shoal waters of some peril, which the Lunenburg schoolmaster determines to navigate despite considerable moral risk.

Assuming that the survival of self is paramount, assuming that we devote ourselves exclusively to security and its law, where does such thinking lead us? Gazing about as he walks from Lunenburg to Halifax, the impending trial of the mutineers much on his mind, Scharf sees hints of the answer everywhere. The red-painted stumps of trees, shorn off by the axes of road-builders enlarging the realm of economic security, seem the handiwork of "blind pirates whose crimes were seen as improvements, whose savagery was reason, and whose violence was Law under which they enslaved themselves and called it freedom." The mercenary attitude of the rural innkeeper, turning his farm into a more profitable shelter for transients, suggests the demeanor of one accepting economic bondage, enslaved like the *Saladin* mutineers by the lure of money, "slave to a master who was substanceless." The shabby condition of hardscrabble farmsteads along the road conveys the impression of self-imposed incarceration, the "gray occupants" toiling in industrious futility, "their walls became their life, inhabited by the ghostly prisoners of their own judgment and choice." Viewed from this ominous perspective, even the capital city's imposing Court House becomes a citadel of frightening implications.

The *Saladin* mutineers are being tried, Scharf comes to realize, not to satisfy the requirements of justice, but in fact to answer the dictates of security. The Attorney-General, in his summation of prosecution, "stated that British Commerce, growing as it had been, needed the protection of the Law." To secure that protection, the mutineers must hang, as testimony to the long reach of the law. But that long reach depended upon the existence of the entire apparatus of commercial government, Admiralty Court, Chief Justice, Attorney-General, soldiers, marines, jailers and all, which in turn existed solely for the punishment of crime against economic security. "Without crime," Scharf reflects uneasily, "needless to say, there would be no court;" and he watches with increasing apprehension as Chief Justice Haliburton pronounces the sentence of death upon the four mutineers who first responded to Fielding's command, noting keenly that murder is once again to be committed in the name of security. The Chief Justice "sought the treasure of safety in their guilt as they sought the *Saladin's* treasure in their mutiny; but all shared the desire for survival as they all shared the guilt." The incongruity of these proceedings is underscored by the Court's failure to convict Carr and Galloway of any crime: the counsel for defense, pleading "fear compelled men to perform acts of desperation," won acquittal on those grounds – a successful plea only driving home the savage desperation of everything else enacted under the rule of security's Law.

"What a trial it has been, from beginning, if it had one, to end, if it does," Scharf muses. "I have reached the Line with the court by means of it and the *Saladin*." This is a man who has travelled too far, and who has seen too much. Like Adam, he has tasted of the fruit of the tree of knowledge, and now views that tree in a more awesome light. His metaphorical sense of acuity haunts him as he paces through the streets of Halifax, following at a discreet distance the melancholy progress of the condemned to the gallows. At the appointed place and hour, situated at the heart of "a grove of young trees" in macabre parody of Eden, stood "the tree of knowledge" fashioned out of security's law. It was, Scharf recognized, "the tree I had envisioned in the court as I watched the Chief Justice and his gardeners cultivate it and bring it to fruition." With its "four vertically hanging tendrils," each "a tear-drop shaped now empty loop, the void circlet that is the only edible product this tree of safety provides," the gibbet-tree "looked grotesque, severely geometrical, a mad-man's dream of what a tree might look like after he, in his madness, had forgotten the trees he had once seen but no longer could." Awaiting the condemned in grave enclave arc four functionaries garbed in black, the High Sheriff, two men of the cloth and the executioner, "like black birds of prey perched in the branches of a tree they designed and built." Soon enough, once each functionary had performed the duties of his office, "the drop was removed and the golden apples attached to the vertical tendrils dropped heavily and swung, gently writhing .... food for the Chief Justice's table."

Scarf doesn't spare himself or us throughout this journal, his often agonized recounting of perceptions, the log of his terrifying voyage. For himself and for us, he merges in identity with others in this forbidding history of a doomed ship, recreating events so terrible they should never be forgotten. "We were following the last vestige of the *Saladin*," he confesses, reliving the memory of pacing along behind the wagons of the condemned. "My shadow and I had boarded her, inventoried her cargo, listened to her Captain Johnston tell his tale which his men corroborated; and now we had returned to her remains from the court to see her a last time and also see, perhaps, her treasures at last." Strange treasures indeed, the cruel and deceptive glitterings of the gold of security, winking and blinking at us through the many diverse scrabblings of humanity after survival.

The most poignant image of this most poignant book is Scarf's account of the final plunge of the *Saladin*, slipping from the rocks of Harbour Island into the trackless deep. This is an image necessarily seen by us in imagination through the eyes of Solomon Scharf, himself seeing in imagination through the eyes of Captain Abraham Cunningham, the last commander of a smashed vessel of forlorn and desperate hopes.

> Her hull was now breached in several places and the guano she carried had leaked out and coloured the sea around her in a shroud of pale, luminous whiteness, a ghostly and chilling sight.... The sea she once floated so proudly upon had entered her, had engulfed her within and without; as the rocks had devoured her hull with their teeth, so now I saw the sea swallow her – she drowned, sliding

into the waters and so lost to my sight forever, hidden in the ocean's maw. All that remained as we left her site on the reef off our starboard quarter was the luminous shroud that marked her grave.... My shadow was gone; I survived and lived on; only the consciousness of her remained, the other watch from which I would not escape.

Thanks to the creative gifts of Henry Sayward Whittier, a former naval officer transmuting himself into a teacher who sometimes talks and sometimes writes, this is an image that should long linger over the ever-broadening expanse of Canadian literature in English.

Wilfred Cude, M.A.
Publisher, MLP